THE CROSS OF
FRANKENSTEIN

THE CROSS OF FRANKENSTEIN

BY
ROBERT J. MYERS

HAMISH HAMILTON
LONDON

First published in Great Britain 1975
by Hamish Hamilton Ltd
90 Great Russell Street London WC1B 3PT

Copyright © 1975 by Robert J. Myers

SBN 241 89245 7

Printed and bound in Great Britain by
BP/E REDWOOD BURN LIMITED
Trowbridge & Esher

TO
ELIZABETH

PREFACE

ONE OF THE MOST intriguing and haunting stories I have ever read is Mary Shelley's *Frankenstein, or The Modern Prometheus*. Some critics find it a poorly constructed novel. Perhaps. I found it satisfying on many levels. First, the situation in which she wrote the story—a young girl with her lover, later her husband, Percy Bysshe Shelley, spending a summer in Switzerland in the early 1800s near their friend and constant companion, Lord Byron. Over a log fire in their quarters on a cool, rainy night, they entertained themselves with German ghost stories. Each agreed to write a ghost story for their mutual entertainment, but only Mary Shelley, aged nineteen, with editorial assistance from her husband, produced one.

Second, the combination of fantasy and horror came off for me in such a highly agreeable manner that I was reluctant for the book to end. Given the character of the monster, it raised speculation in my mind as to whether her conclusion was really the end of the affair. Briefly, the monster left the ship in the Arctic, after viewing his creator's corpse, to return to his ice raft and vanish into the Arctic night, having pledged that he would perish on a funeral pyre in the northernmost part of the earth and that his ashes would be swept away by the sea.

The success of her story stems from her development of the character and intellect of the monster so that he becomes the most fascinating of the whole cast. The keenness of his mind, his cleverness and deceitfulness, his superhuman power to withstand cold, for example, and to run and climb made him a formidable creature. It seemed out of character for such a monster, however, to have simply finished himself off. There were still worlds to conquer, and his most determined antagonist was dead.

Most Americans still equate the monster with Frankenstein, the creator. The old movie monster merely grunts. Mary Shelley's monster, on the other hand, succeeded in educating himself during his many travels and, in revenge for his creator's thoughtlessness in making him hideous and abandoning him, retaliated against Frankenstein, plotting one personal tragedy after another. The basic idea of her story, the impulse toward crossing the frontiers of morality in the name of unrestricted creativity, remains as powerful as ever. We can look at such technological advances as nuclear fission and the cloning process in biology, as well as the consequences of such everyday inventions as the automobile and electric home heating; all these things in our own day point up the paradox of evil arising from good. Modern Promethean spirits are still very much on the scene.

The idea of trying to extend the story into another era has been in my mind for about six years. I thought of it while reading her book again at the time of the television broadcasts of the first flight to the moon, and Neil Armstrong's "One small step for a man, one giant leap for mankind." Who knows, for example, what will come out of space exploration? Then in the fall of 1973 I read the book once more to find material for a talk I was giving to college students on *The Tragedy of King Richard II*, another Promethean character. In October 1973, with the story of Frankenstein and his monster very much on my mind, I took a trip to my favorite camping ground, the wilderness area of Dolly Sods near Petersburg, West Virginia. It was there, by myself, huddling in the cold by a fitful campfire, that I started this continuation of Mary Shelley's story. I returned in August 1974 and experienced a powerful storm of rain and thunder and lightning.

Meanwhile, others were at work on diverse variations of the Frankenstein theme. In late 1973 there was an original television production, *Frankenstein, the True Story*, by Christopher Isherwood and Don Bachardy. While I take exception to the title (Mary Shelley's version to me is still the True Story), the changes were effective and the story they told was as exciting as the original. Critical attention to Mary Shelley's writing of the story appeared in a new annotated edition of *Frankenstein* edited by James H. Rieger (Bobbs-Merrill, 1974). And in the summer of 1974 there was a novel, *Frankenstein Unbound*, by Brian W. Aldiss, a science fiction story taking the author to Switzerland during the original events (Random House). And then came Andy Warhol's movie, *Frankenstein*, followed by Mel Brooks's comedy, *Young Frankenstein*.

Despite all the imagination and ingenuity that have so far been applied to this marvelous story, there is still room, I believe, to bring this legend to America, where it may survive and grow.

I appreciate the opportunity to present this continuation of the Frankenstein legend in the land where the original Mary Shelley story first appeared and hope that the British audience will enjoy equally this Americanized sequel recorded by Frankenstein's illegitimate son after living for many years in the United States.

ROBERT J. MYERS

Washington, D.C.
October 1974

CONTENTS

PREFACE vii

CHAPTER

    I. DISCOVERY 1

    II. THE VISITOR 17

    III. KIDNAPED 37

    IV. BERKELEY SPRINGS 55

    V. THE DOWNS 73

    VI. THE CULT 87

    VII. FLIGHT 104

    VIII. CAPTURED 125

    IX. THE EVE OF RESURRECTION 144

    X. TREACHERY 164

    XI. THE CHASE 184

    XII. THE FLAWED ESCAPE 194

Farewell remorse! All good to me is lost;
Evil, be thou my good . . .

—Paradise Lost

THE CROSS OF
FRANKENSTEIN

CHAPTER I

DISCOVERY

"WHAT'S IN A NAME?" *Romeo and Juliet* is not my favorite Shakespearean tragedy. I mention this only to register my disagreement with that general proposition. Names do make a good deal of difference. It was my surname, specifically, that had become an obsession with me as I labored long and hard in my medical career, bearing instead the surname of my "Aunt" Margaret Saville, who, out of the Lord's providence, had raised me from a child. My gratitude was diminished by my conviction that, for lo those many years, there were things—that is to say, information and events—that should have been made known to me, but were somehow smothered against the great breast of Aunt Margaret, who had known only a few years of marital bliss before Major Saville had fallen in an obscure conflict on the outer edge of Empire. And so she looked toward her brother, the renowned mariner Captain Robert Walton, for succor from the ambivalent joys of widowhood and had, on his behalf, for almost forty years maintained a splendid town house on Salisbury

Square in London. This was my home, a place of comfort and beauty, a tribute to the unremitting toil and risks of four generations of Waltons in their pursuit of the goods of this world in the most dangerous trade winds.

My gratitude, as I say, was less than it might have been when my Aunt Margaret, with many sighs and tears, advised me of my fateful heritage. "Victor, dear, you are now past sixteen, and it is my duty to tell you of your origin. You know you are adopted—you understand all of that, and why we love you so. That is the simple part. But at your age, as you approach the threshold of manhood, you must know from whence you came and what that means to you as you make your own way."

I realized the strain on her natural sensitivities such a statement required. She had up to that time completely nourished me with her concern and supervision, save for summer outings in Scotland, where my love of hills and rivers multiplied like the spawning salmon. I did not know, however, that, compared to the future strain on me, her burden was in reality nothing.

Up to that time I had lived a simple and secure life, tutored in the classics, Greek and Latin, and the poetry of Shakespeare, Milton, and Wordsworth. I also studied natural philosophy, or science, as an antidote to too much classical study. And my curiosity was aroused by such diverse subjects as alchemy and the works and writings of George Ripley. As time passed, it was in the study of natural and living organisms that I excelled, even though Aunt Margaret herself encouraged me in other directions.

It was shortly before I was to enter Eton that she decided upon revelation. It was a mellow September day. The year was 1816, for I was born not too many months before the turn of the new century, on June 23. Diffused sunlight poured down on the garden just outside, and the room glinted from the embossed leather bindings of the Captain's handsome library. Captain Walton had died the previous winter while commanding a cargo of cotton from America, when he was swept from the bridge by a sudden, massive wave that rose from the ocean depths, struck, and was gone.

"I pledged the Captain that when you became sixteen, you should know the full story of your parents." Her vision clouded and, as though in sympathy, the outside clouded too, casting the room in a somber late afternoon light. I felt weak.

"You should know that your father was a genius, a scientist who with good fortune would have been linked with such men as Dr. William Harvey and the rest. And he was so kind and charming, the kind of friend the Captain had been searching for all his life. It was tragic that their friendship was of such short duration. I have here this packet of letters, sent to me by the Captain years ago from the frozen wastes of the Arctic for safekeeping. They tell the whole story of your father's unusual career and the tragedies that befell him and his entire family, save for you and your dear mother."

She paused to compose herself. Her gold-framed oval glasses slipped further down her plump and pleasant nose as she daubed at her eyes with a folded forefinger. "Read these letters carefully. Study them thoughtfully, and when you finish, let us discuss any problems that they raise for you. I suggest that you read them in private and keep the information in them to yourself. I think you will understand once you see what they have to say."

With that she handed me a packet of letters wrapped in a blue silk kerchief and excused me from the library. I went up the great winding stairs to my room with a pounding heart. I had often heard allusions to my father in conversations between my aunt and the Captain, but all queries about him were met with the story that he had died in the Arctic before my birth, that he was a scientist from Switzerland, and that all his family had long been dead. Now I was to find out who he was, put flesh on the phantom I had so often conjured up. My aunt felt that she was doing the proper thing. I am now not so certain, but then, as I was to learn, she had no choice but to tell me of the past, for it was the only way in the end that I had an opportunity to cope with the future. In any case, I found that my family name was Frankenstein, a name I learned to bear in pride and terror.

Let me be as brief as possible, from reading, rereading—yes, memorizing—those incredible letters. My father's fascination at school with the natural philosophies led him to study works long discredited, but somehow, in the crucible of his mind, he found the secret of creation and could not resist the temptation to implement it. This is badly put, but it strikes the essence of the matter. There was nothing in Captain Walton's letters about the details of the experiments themselves, although there is the immediate conjecture that they were meticulously recorded. Here is what the letters actually said on this point: "Some miracle might have produced it, yet the stages of the discovery were distinct and probable. After days and nights of incredible labour and fatigue, I succeeded in discovering the cause of generation and life; nay, more, I became myself capable of bestowing animation upon lifeless matter."

One can only surmise that he could not have been confident, finally, of success, or it is inexplicable why he would have brought to life a creature by his own description of terrible proportions and grotesque features. A confident creator, a modern Prometheus, would have shaped something on a lesser but perfect scale and, in accomplishing such a feat, would have certainly wished to have gained full recognition in the scientific community of that day. But that was not to be. When my father saw the "dull yellow eye" blink and a shudder of animation course through the creature's body, he fled into the night and fell into a sickness and fever that nearly claimed his life. I can only speculate that the enormity of what he had done—the creation of a work of the Devil—left so great a weight on his mind and soul that he temporarily lost his senses. That explanation is easy to entertain if one can believe that he accomplished the first—that is, the creation of a living being from inanimate matter, the dead flesh of animals of all descriptions—so I am convinced.

I emphasize the point of authenticity of this Monster, partly, I suppose, in an effort to explain it away to a natural cause and thus escape my share of inherited guilt for unleashing such a terrible force into this already troubled world. There is, for example, the height (eight feet) and abnormally fast running ability, associated with the reports of a snow monster that is supposed to inhabit the snow-clad and hostile mountains of Asia. I had read of this possibility, the theory that such a creature, perhaps a derivation from a large ape, might be involved in the original work. But the accounts of Captain Walton's discussions with my father, to be fair, rule out the possibility that the Monster was anything other than my father's creation. For some time after his animation, nearly two years, the Monster simply vanished. Then there was the strangling murder of my father's young brother, William, and the circumstantial clue that led to the false accusation and hanging of our servant, Justine, for that crime, which she did not commit. My father knew intuitively that the Monster had struck. Sometime later, in a desolated place in the Alps, their first conversation took place. The Monster had almost miraculously survived. He had educated himself through hiding and living in a shed adjoining the cottage of a family in the countryside, and in this way had realized his condition. His plea to my father was so poignant that to this day I can recite it word for word. "Remember, that I am thy creature; I ought to be thy Adam; but I am rather the fallen angel, whom thou drivest from joy for no misdeed. Everywhere I see bliss, from which I alone am irrevocably excluded. I was benevolent and good; misery made me a fiend. Make me happy, and I shall again be virtuous."

Yet there was the fact of the murders and the demand that my father fashion a mate for him, upon a guarantee that he would remove himself to the jungles of Brazil and there uncoil his life in harmless bucolic pursuits. In exchange, he would cease his pursuit of my father's destruction by the despoiling of all that was dear and slack his passion in a different way. The temptation to do this deed was so strong that my father went to an isolated Orkney island to fulfill this odious obligation, but finally, overcome with remorse and fearful of the weight of responsibility if he compounded his initial error, my father terminated that work, disposing of the remains in the sea. The Fiend, seeing all this happen, took quick revenge against my father's closest friend, murdering him that very night.

This experience further ravaged my father's mental and moral equilibrium. At last he returned to his home in Switzerland and married his childhood sweetheart, despite the Monster's threat that he would "see him on his wedding night." Fully armed, my father awaited the Monster's coming, only to find the blow struck not at him, but at his bride. On the graves of the Monster's victims, my father, Victor Frankenstein, swore vengeance on the Monster and devoted the remaining years of his life to running him down, throughout the countries of Europe, the Middle East, and the Far North. The Monster remained strangely content with this pursuit, aiding my father in finding the trail, mocking him, keeping him alive by guiding him to food, for example—all part of the torture and penitence that the Monster considered his due. My father's death on Captain Walton's icebound ship left the Monster with no further goal in life, and his last statement to Captain Walton was his determination to build a funeral pyre in the furthermost reaches of the North, with his ashes swept into the sea. The last view Captain Walton had of the Monster was the raft disappearing into the darkness of the Arctic night.

This is only a summary of these magnificent letters. This brief account is not adequate to the tale, and it in no way describes the acute, sometimes exquisite, torture that the reading of this tale had on my innocent mind. I read on and on, missing dinner altogether. The butler,

William, quietly lighted the lamps and candles, and my aunt discreetly left me to myself, pondering the meaning of all of this.

So it was not until the next morning, after breakfast, that she again called me into the library. Sunk into her favorite brocaded chair, with her gray hair tied in a tight bun and her oval glasses sliding down over her nose, she wore a somber face to match the plainness of her brown ankle-length woolen dress.

"I hope you slept well, Victor," she said in a tone which assumed that I had not. And in fact that was true. My dreams had been wild and disjointed, murky and dreadful, and it had been a relief to waken fully with the dawn and think again about this heritage in the light of day in a familiar place.

"The point that bothers me most, Aunt Margaret, is that I do not see how I am a part of this. I am not mentioned in the letters at all."

"Quite right. There is no mention of you at all in those letters. There was one other letter, to your mother, that Captain Walton sent on at your father's request, which is how she came to us with you shortly thereafter. It was during your father's pursuit of the Fiend through Europe that your father met your mother, a simple tavern maid in Hamburg. Having again lost the Monster's trail for some weeks, your father stayed in the inn, and it was at this time that you were conceived. Some months later, your father, torn between starting a new life or continuing the chase as he had vowed, once again sighted the Fiend at the docks, boarding a ship. His duty clear, he bade farewell to your mother and went to meet his fate."

"But I am confused as to how I am here and not somewhere else altogether."

"I am coming to that point. On his deathbed, your father handed the Captain a letter to send to your mother. The Captain noted the address, and in the next year, when in port at Hamburg, he stopped by. He found your mother in poverty, working to support the two of you. A generous man, he invited her—urged her—to bring you and live with us. The thought was that she would become our cook and raise you in pleasant surroundings. So this was done, but no sooner had she arrived with you in the middle of winter than she fell ill with a virulent case of influenza and passed away within a week. That left you, by God's providence, with me, to raise as my child."

"And my mother's grave?"

"Near Hamburg with her relatives."

"But what of the story? Did such a monster really exist?"

"There seems to be no doubt about it, certainly not in Captain Walton's mind. After all, he saw him, talked with him. The story as it related to the Frankenstein family in Switzerland was publicized only to a small degree. The times he was seen by people generally were fleeting. Now there have been popular stories for years on the Continent about Dr. Frankenstein and his Monster, but they are generally more fiction than truth. The notoriety has assuredly died down. The question was what to do for your own safety. Captain Walton thought it would be most unwise to have it public knowledge that you were Victor Frankenstein's son. One could not be certain that the Monster was dead, or that some old score, unknown to any of us, might be evened against your person. And so you have become a Saville."

"But I am the son of Victor Frankenstein, who created life from the dead?"

"You are indeed. I have worried over this whole affair for years. In one way it is a proud accomplishment of science, although I am opposed to the extent that it appears to be irreverent and against God. Still, there has never been an achievement like your father's since the Resurrection, God save my soul."

To realize that I was the sole remaining spark of that frantic energy, that kind and tortured man who had looked into the very vortex of the universe and had alone succeeded in imitating God and Nature, was as exhilarating as it was depressing. That very act had earned only opprobrium, and its wages were death and disgrace. My impulse was to blurt out my allegiance to my rightful name, become a famous surgeon, and raise high the family escutcheon from the muddy ditch where man's inhumanity, one to the other, had hurled it. I felt a swelling of pride and a general desire to demonstrate to the whole world the power of the mark of Frankenstein. But in sum, my emotions were confused rather than focused.

"I think I sense your thoughts, dear Victor, and I counsel that you wait some time longer before you make your decision. There may well come a propitious moment when that is exactly what you will want to do; that is, reclaim your name. Indeed, you may feel honor bound to do so. But for the nonce, it seems to me that it would only complicate your life." I came to her as she indicated, and she held my two hands and looked deeply into my eyes with her overwhelming love, and I acquiesced in the decision at this point.

I was at the stage of life where most of life's decisions were made for me in any event. This left my mind free to pursue my studies as I made my way through Eton and then into the university and medical school. The name Saville suited me well, and the question of whether I should take up the name Frankenstein lay dormant. Thus I would become Doctor Saville.

The considerable fortune of Aunt Margaret, thanks to Captain Walton's industry, made my school experience comfortable. Oxford was in the mold of the Saville appreciation of the world—conservative and Tory. I followed the events of the day avidly, especially the aftermath in France of the triumph of God and the Duke of Wellington over Napoleon, a victory that had reassured me that good conquers evil. I familiarized myself with the leading political ideas, the works of Jeremy Bentham and his utilitarians. The "greatest happiness for the greatest number" seemed to be the worthy goal of the Anglican Church, but the movement never received support from that area, Bentham concluding that God was not meshed with his utilitarian philosophy. At home on week ends with Aunt Margaret, we would inevitably go to our Anglican church, and although our Bishop clearly seemed more interested in fox hunting than soul saving, I nonetheless shared my aunt's feelings against the dissenters in the Church, the Evangelical movement, that threatened to upset the natural order of things. Of course this was true of utilitarianism too, but it was scientific and I for one could see no way to hold down whatever came of those efforts. In that

I was at one with my father; if he had discovered these laws of life, there was no way of halting the application, any more than turning back and fighting a flood-swollen river. One inevitably went with the current.

The knowledge of my father's accomplishment acted as a powerful intellectual stimulus during my medical student days. I studied the works of Albrecht von Haller on the nature of human substance and the action of the nervous system. I was quick to follow the clinical method of studying the body, anxious to see for myself the effects of disease and the causes of death, particularly cholera, which came with great regularity, especially in the port towns and cities of England. The cause of it was a mystery, associated in some manner with the decay of organic materials that was suspected of putting noxious vapors in the air. I was confident, however, that my profession would solve that mystery and more.

When I was graduated from medical school, I sought an active assignment, but near my aunt and the security of the Saville home and fortune. The local hospital, inspired and built through the efforts of the great surgeon John Hunter, was little more than a mile from our square, the last half mile going through the slums surrounding the cotton mills, where the stench of humanity was so bad, when I was conscious of it, that the whole area smelled like a sick ward. I was proficient at my healing tasks and at surgery, and the years passed constructively enough.

There were two medical subjects that stimulated my interest more than others, and, in the basement of the town house, I constructed a simple laboratory to observe the effect of electric current on the muscle systems of animals, after the experiments of both Luigi Galvani and Alessandro Volta, and the circulation of the blood and the working of the heart valves on veins and arteries as first formulated by Dr. William Harvey. While I had no specific ideas on how one might proceed, I had the strong feeling that if my father's experiment could in any way be repeated, the animating force of electricity and a thorough, or even new, approach to the blood supply in some way had to be involved.

It was these endeavors that brought me more closely into William's path. The butler's quarters were in the basement, comfortable and dry enough, not like the cellars of the slums, and he was curious about my laboratory work and would sometimes come by and sit and watch. He was expected to clean the containers and he did that well. I was indifferent to his presence. I learned more of his background from his soliloquies than I desired to know. Aunt Margaret had been full of good advice on the need to keep one's distance from the lower orders, to avoid becoming involved in a personal way with their problems. This was also part of her desire to preserve me from the possible bad effects of the daily sight of the slum sensuality that was on continuous display and beckoned to me on my route back and forth from the hospital. William was an unusual man for a butler, however, and he let me know it. He had been in his second year at the Royal Military College in Sandhurst, on his way to becoming an artillery officer, when he was painfully kicked by a horse in the head and knee, ending his military career. He walked with a limp, quite decidedly on damp days, and the scar on his temple was only partly covered by his thinning brownish hair. He read the pamphlets of the day, everything from Tom Paine to socialist tracts, and he was devoted, he said, to the idea of a wider voting franchise.

"The order of things, William," I had to say at last, "is preordained, and this tampering with our traditions and government just will not do. It is not difficult to think of a set of circumstances far more difficult for us all than those under King George and the Tory government. Uncertainty, change—those are things to be avoided."

His military training left him powerless to argue directly. I could tell that he not only did not agree, but also felt that his post now was beneath his rightful station.

"But what of science itself, sir?"

"Science follows natural paths of evolution, as established by God. It tells us more about ourselves—helps cure the ill, for example. A force for good."

"And science and religion?"

"Science simply helps explain religion," I lied. The literal interpretation of the Bible bothered me a good deal, for I could foresee, and my imagination was not on the leading edge of the whole subject, that a clash was inevitable. Not, one would hope, before Aunt Margaret's death, for she would never be up to it.

"If you succeed in what you are trying to do," said William, "what then of the Creation?"

I stopped abruptly. Aunt Margaret had never intimated that William knew anything about my father's work. Of course he could have surreptitiously found the letters years ago, or recently, and read some of them, or even the whole packet. But I ignored that. "I'm trying to do nothing but help cure sick people." I turned my back on him, and he limped from the laboratory with a nasty chuckle.

Late at night, well after midnight, I went by the library and poured myself a sherry. The new butt from Portugal was excellent, and it was a pleasure to the nose and palate. I thought for the thousandth time, Where were my father's scientific notebooks that would have contained the results of his experiments for posterity? Had they been included in the materials Captain Walton had sent? If not, where were they? Would they not still exist? The fire was dying, the good oak coals red and angry. I was now almost thirty—over twenty-eight, to be precise—and while I was not unhappy with my medical career and the good I believed I did and the knowledge I was accumulating, this was not really enough. I had allowed myself to wander off on a side lane, clung to Aunt Margaret and her motherly love to keep me in a kind of mindless comfort, taking advantage of my medical interests so that I avoided most of society. I scarcely knew a lady of my own class, for example, except those casually met at church, who, without a special effort on my part, would remain beyond my reach. At the same time I had this obsession—for I had to face up that there was no other word for it—that somehow in my desultory scientific experimentation, enlightenment would come over me. I really wanted to reconstruct my father's experiment, without the horrible unwanted collateral results. I wanted to be able to help man perfect himself, "the greatest happiness for the greatest number," not the deformed and starving wretches that I passed daily on the muddy streets of their death-ridden slum, but superior people who could do superior work. Surely that was a worthy goal, and one that God could hardly take exception to. It was knowing that such a thing was possible that was tearing me apart. Lately, I was subject to sudden and massive headaches that kept me to my chambers.

It was April, and a spring rain was dripping down the leaded windowpanes. Earlier in the day I had walked through the gardens, savoring the overwhelming ammonia smell of the boxwood and the freshness of the grass. It was a time of flux of the seasons, and a critical point in my life.

CHAPTER II

THE VISITOR

THREE DAYS AFTER my midnight ruminations I
received an unsettling caller. It was an hour or so after I
had returned from the hospital and had settled down in
the library, as was my custom. A coal fire sputtered. The
fire would improve, I knew, as the evening wore on, so
I ignored the occasional puffs of smoke. The leather-
covered chair in which I sat near the fire was across from
the brocaded one beloved by my aunt. My chair was so
situated that it would catch the heat, and I was rarely
bothered by the drafts and changes in outside temperatures that worked their way into the serenity of the library. The velvet draperies were drawn, and the heavy
Oriental carpets seemed to brighten themselves for my
comfort. The brass fireplace fixtures had at no time
seemed so polished and hospitable. Aunt Margaret had
taken the carriage early to attend to a problem of a distant
relative of her husband's, an Evangelical minister named
McInnes. She had been extremely agitated the previous
day, but she had not confided the specifics to me. Instead,

she had wept copiously and frowned until her oval glasses had almost fallen off the end of her nose. She had risen with the dawn and disappeared.

I lighted my clay pipe from a candle on the mantel and began to dream about my father. I had been in this semitrance for perhaps ten minutes when William crept upon my consciousness. Not intruded, mind you, for he would never do that. He was somehow able to insinuate himself into whatever situation, do his duty, and then be on his way.

"Doctor," he said, "there is a gentleman who insists upon seeing you. I suggested that he leave his card for another time, but he persisted. He alleges, sir, that he was a friend of Captain Walton's." With that, William presented a calling card: "Frederick Greene, Chandler, Baltimore, Maryland."

No business had I with the shipping industry, no less with a chandler, a merchant who worked his way back and forth between wharf and ship in search of a pound. Yes, of course, some had done uncommonly well and were on the way toward inheriting the earth. But if he had been a friend of the late Captain's . . .

"I know of no one of that name, William, but in deference to my uncle, please show him in."

William ushered in the stranger, and we eyed each other curiously. I motioned to him to take my aunt's chair. He appeared at ease, familiar with social life. His eyes were bright and his cheeks slightly flushed, presumably from the wind on this blustery evening. On that assumption, I offered him a sherry, which he accepted. He was thin, wiry, perhaps fifty years old, about six feet tall, with a straight thin nose, thinning reddish hair, and dark brown eyes which reflected the fire. A gold watch chain crossed his velvet waistcoat. His coat and breeches were of good gray wool, with an older, one might say Colonial, cut. He was mild and polite in his demeanor. Though at ease, he was alert like a cat. He adjusted and arranged himself several times in the chair and then addressed himself to the purpose of his visit.

"I come on a mission for a client," the chandler said, "and with reluctance do I impose on an old friendship."

"If your problem is within my power to solve, I shall be pleased to consider it," I replied, unsettled by the oddness of his appearance, his Yankee accent (if that was what it was), the brightness of his eyes.

"The request has to do with a certain chemical formula, which, I hope, will be compounded by you."

"But I am not an apothecary, simply a physician."

"Yet remembering the good Captain, there is the possibility that you will bring to the formula a solution that has so far eluded the apothecary shops of Baltimore."

I looked at the stranger more closely. The slightly out-of-style impression that he had originally created in my mind was reinforced by small, yet salient, features. For instance, the lace collar was typical of an era some time past, I suspect, even in America, and the cloth of his breeches had a certain coarseness that is difficult to define. His mud-stained boots, too, though sturdy enough and designed to keep the feet dry, looked old, although not much worn. And the face. That is where I at last saw it. There was a distinct unevenness of features between the right- and left-hand halves of the face, beyond what I would consider normal. I stood and looked in the mirror above the fireplace, refilling my pipe, to observe my own visage, to note the position of the ear lobes, the eyebrows, the height of the cheekbones. Different, yes, but not in the same way as Mr. Greene's features.

"There may be rewards in the solution of this formula," he continued, "that would be unique for you. A puzzle that you above all might solve."

I gave my brightest and most arch look. There was a suggestion here of the illegal, the idea that somehow I was to participate in, say, some aspects of the opium trade, which I found most vile. The activity of my own government at this very moment in the Orient sickened me as a human being and heightened my distaste for the whole subject.

"I trust that my giving you a hearing has not led you to the conclusion that I am anything but what I am—a God-fearing general practitioner. I will not be a party to putting my name to a formula that is not actually needed by a particular patient. I fail completely to understand your suggestion."

Mr. Greene became pensive, perhaps confused, as though the mere mention of his request on behalf of his unidentified client would be quite sufficient, all that he had been prepared to expect. So when I raised the necessary objection—necessary in terms of my profession and my pride—he seemed unable to continue.

He raised his head again, as though he had been thinking ponderous thoughts. "Very well," he said, "though your refusal is perhaps premature. I may have stated the matter badly. As I said, the formula is one that somehow has eluded the apothecaries of Baltimore. There is indeed, I am told, nothing illicit about it. It is, in fact, a humanitarian request."

With that he fumbled in his inner coat pocket and produced a bulging leather case. From it he extracted a page of foolscap and handed it over to me.

"Once you absorb this, the problem will, I hope, be clearer."

I accepted the worn piece of ruled paper and unfolded it. It was written in a crabbed but careful hand. The heading was "The Fluid," and it explained that careful attention was required for its preparation. At first glance the formula seemed to be that of formaldehyde or some such noxious chemical, but the differences were significant. Mr. Greene waited for me to speak, observing like a bird of prey my every reaction, from hand to eye. He seemed to be mentally recording this moment for later transmission.

"What my client requests is for you to procure the various compounds in this formula from Swiss or German suppliers in London. He feels that the American equivalents slightly miss the mark and the combination of small differences is causing difficulty."

"I would like to know more about your client, if I may. Is he a doctor, or a chemist, or precisely what?"

"I have not yet met him for a variety of reasons and am in communication but indirectly. It is my understanding that he is in need of this fluid. But the problem so far is the viscosity. It does not congeal properly." He added more details that I would recall later.

"So what you desire is for me to produce this fluid from the formula. But how it will turn out, I have no way to tell."

"If you will do this—that is, make an experimental batch—I will take it back with me, and once it is tested by my client, we can confer again. There may then be matters of importance that could develop to our mutual benefit, using much larger quantities." He caught himself, as though in hindsight he had misspoken.

"But Mr. Greene," I said once again, "why were you sent to me?"

"I was told that you would understand what was involved, and that you would most likely prefer that this matter be handled by you and not by others. I was told that this formula is a kind of blood substitute."

I was relieved and exhilarated that he had said that. But mixed with those feelings was a new element: the desire for revenge. Under the guise of cooperating, I might find the means to strike back at these strange forces, whose identity I instantly suspected. I tried to keep that idea in check, for the perspiration that stood in tiny beads on my forehead was neither from the fire nor from the sherry. The discovery of a substitute for blood must have been the key to my father's phenomenal success. It accounted for the strength, even the eating habits, of the Monster, his ability to withstand cold. Did this formula come from the missing notebooks? The Fiend might well have taken them from the ship perhaps, but if he had not burned on a funeral pyre, he surely was lost among the ice floes in the harsh weather. One would assume that his great bulk might have been discovered, half rotted or devoured by wild beasts, and the notebooks secured by a passing whaler, a missionary, natives, fur traders. The notebooks themselves, in knowing hands, would be worth a fortune, a phenomenon to present to the world, the work of my father, Dr. Victor Frankenstein. Recognition and fame at last. I wanted those notebooks. They were mine. And I wanted to punish those who had, for so long, kept those possessions from my rightful grasp.

"This request is so unusual that I really do not know how to respond," I said instead. "I would like some time to think about it."

"Suppose I return in a week?" said Greene.

I nodded.

Mr. Greene drained his sherry, arose, and departed from the room. I accompanied him to the door of the drawing room, William being visible now in the hall with Mr. Greene's coat, hat, and stout-looking cane. We shook hands briefly. His hands were still cold, despite the time spent before the fire. "Dress warmly," I said, "or the London cold will settle in your bones." He gave me his thin smile, slipped into his greatcoat, smiled again, waved his broad-brimmed hat, and disappeared into the night. There was a cold feeling in the hall and part way into the drawing room. I repaired to the library, anxious to resume my study of that single sheet of paper.

But there was little more there than the complex formula. How I longed to obtain the whole work, if indeed my supposition was correct. There was no reason to think that Mr. Greene would have the records or, for that matter, know of their existence. But surely the possessor knew what he had. The fact that he was apparently considering compounding it showed either a need or a plan, or both. But where and for what purpose? I had made no commitment, I told myself, to do anything. I would see what happened with the formula, certainly. I would do that in any case. If I could find the records, the notebooks, it would not be, I rationalized, for the sake of repeating the experiment—even then that thought welled in my brain and almost caused the sherry glass to slip from my grasp—but for its value to the scientific world. What value, though, without an exhibit to prove the potency of this startling work?

The beauty of the formula was its simplicity. How strange is the brain of man, the difference between the ordinary and the genius. These same simple symbols written in any other order or quantity would produce nothing of value, but under the hand of my father they had produced the life-giving flow. Synthetic blood? Not suitable for human beings, but precisely correct for the pseudo man he had created!

The next evening I returned from the hospital with the full collection of chemicals, produced in Germany, and three samples of blood taken from patients that day. Still no news from Aunt Margaret. I explained casually to William that I was going to do some laboratory work at home for two special and serious cases, not wanting to wait for the usual and haphazard proceedings that often took place in the hospital's laboratory. With the formula at hand, there was not as much demand on my chemistry skills as I had first imagined, and within three hours the batch was brewed, hot and steamy, a darker shade than blood, more viscous, and with a decidedly more pungent smell than human or animal blood. How my admiration for, and curiosity about, my father soared! It was as though he had come to my presence through this single formula, this sheet of paper. His imagination and genius had broken into new areas of human capability, but had not achieved understanding or acceptance. The idea of making a living being was so repugnant to the humanity of his day (and certainly my own) that it was no wonder those who dared conceive these dramatic moves, against the grain of popular understanding, were destined to suffer. As surely had my father. My very repetition of his experiment with a life-giving fluid filled me with the same elation and apprehension that had no doubt filled his mind at the same moment fifty years before.

As the mixture cooled, it retained its intense purple color, and only then did I begin to think of how I should store it until Mr. Greene's return. It was now gelatinlike, and I was thinking of pouring the whole mixture into a porcelain bowl as a preliminary to deciding how it should be prepared for the long journey to America—to Baltimore—where there was a demand for it. I watched the congealing process for a few moments longer, but then, to my surprise, the congealing ceased and the mass began to disintegrate, the mixture breaking down and flowing into the bottom of the flask, like inexpensive wine. Within a few minutes, the whole experiment was in a watery liquid state. The congealed mass had, of course, been equally inconceivable, but the viscosity of it made sense, because the dilute residue I now had would run out of an opening in a system like water, there apparently being nothing that would slow it in any way.

Thoughts raced through my mind like so many snowflakes. Someone wanted synthetic blood, had the formula, but was unable to manufacture it or to find anyone who could. So that intelligence had hit upon the idea—the thought or obsession—that the solution lay in Europe, the land of the original creation, that somehow the chemicals and the water abroad would reproduce the magic elixir, and that the son of Frankenstein would be inspired, in the hollow of his sweaty hands, to reproduce that miracle.

(Had Captain Walton unfolded the tale of Frankenstein to an enthralled audience in some Maryland tavern, including the chandler?) The result, though, was quite obviously a failure. If I presented that to Mr. Greene, he would take it, but once it reached its destination, my failure would be apparent. And with that failure would go the prospect of recovering my father's notebooks and the secret of creation. I had known before, and I knew then, that the possession of that secret might well be fatal or drive me mad. But on the other hand, knowledge of this legacy, and now the clue that the original research was still extant, excited me wildly. I lay on the brick floor of my cellar in a stupor and sweat, oblivious to the cold and the hour.

So it was in the grayness of the dawn, the lifting of the heavy velvet veil of night, that I more or less recovered my senses and rose unsteadily from the floor. The apparatus stood in mockery of my efforts, and the liquid still stood in the decanter. My candles had guttered down dangerously, and the smells of the chemicals had combined to produce a heavy and nauseous aroma that was building a massive headache just behind my tortured and bloodshot eyes. The decanter was only a few inches from a large and sputtering candle, and in an instant I realized that I might have the answer. I removed the decanter from the table and placed it on the cellar window sill, where the full benefit of the cracks brought in the cold winter air. Cold alone might cause it to congeal to some extent. The heat might have destroyed the texture. I waited patiently for the liquid to cool down so that I could see what the results might be.

What was the problem? This surged through my

mind like a gigantic pounding wave, striking at the roots of my senses and sensibilities. With the Fiend long disposed of, someone else had come into possession of the notebooks and the story of the success of the experiment, and, through the mysterious agency of Mr. Greene, was determined to work out the whole vile process again, perhaps on a larger scale. But the fluid, the essence of the work, had baffled the person or persons, for without a substance to sustain the life functions, no matter of creation, however clever and inspired, would survive. Those involved would only have been moved in the extreme to send a messenger to me in London. So their knowledge was exact and their conviction extraordinary to take that chance, if chance it was—that is, knowing what I did, I might well have summoned the authorities to determine what Greene represented. But they must have counted on my curiosity or the vagueness of any charge I could hurl. There was, after all, something insolent and supercilious about the strange fellow who had shown up. I hated myself for such an obvious self-weakness that others, whoever they were, had seen it and had capitalized on it with confidence.

Dawn had come. It was nearly eight o'clock. I approached the window sill and raised the flask toward the window. I looked through sleep-laden eyes into the contents and slowly turned the bottle about. Failure. The contents were, if anything, thinner than they had been when I subjected them to the cold of the window sill. I placed the decanter back on the workbench, tapped the cork firmly into place, and made my way to the health and civilization of the drawing room. I went on into the hall and started up the stairs, where William appeared from the woodwork and smiled and said, "Good morning, sir." I grunted and more or less fled up the stairway to my bedroom. It was as though I had come back into the house after an evening of grave robbing. I could see no patients that day; I felt feverish. I rang the bell and when William arrived, I apprised him of my condition, issued orders to my office at the hospital, and ordered absolute silence and rest for myself. I was unable to carry that out, however, as I lay in my bed tossing and turning, sweating and chilling, racked by the mystery and by my conscience and undefined feelings of rage and anxiety.

The sleep during the morning was fairly restful, but soon came the headache with apparitions and shadows and flashes like magic slides of Greene and the vision of my father and the Monster, who rose like a volcanic bubble. I shouted out more than once, but each time recovered and fell back in the bed. It was not until four in the afternoon that I awoke, exhausted, but with the fever gone and the headache better, and the lightness in the head associated with a lack of rest and food and a troubled soul. I rang William for my bath and, after ablution, began to recover my composure. Wearing my slippers and silk smoking jacket, I went down the circular stairs and took my accustomed place by the fire, where my evening sherry was already laid out. My aunt had not been heard from, indicating the lack of resolution of her mission. I sipped my sherry and felt the perspiration break out once again on my forehead. Without looking, I could tell that William was in the dark of the hall, viewing me with concern. He had the Devil's own intuition. There was no way I could dissemble anything from him.

My mind turned now like a torch on the problem of

the purple fluid, and everything else was in darkness. If the results were as unsatisfactory to Greene as I was certain they would be to his masters, my role in the affair might be ended, and I would be left forever to ponder the reason for this strange request, and puzzle over the prospect that someone had it in his power, or nearly in his power, to create a whole race or subcategory of the human species, sensate creatures that could think, and run, and yes, kill. Could they reproduce? The idea had intrigued me from the early readings of my father's research and the Fiend's desire for a mate. Could it be that the construction of two such beings, with different sex characteristics, could result in the ability of these monsters to reproduce themselves? There was really no reason to suppose that this would be impossible, if one could accept the idea that it was possible to create such a being in the first instance. But should I be a party to helping in whatever was going on for whatever purposes, by a group I had every reason to distrust—even to fear?

The blood, the purple fluid, was my immediate concern. It simply could not be so thin and runny, I thought, and yet accomplish the purpose of blood in the human system as I understood it. I had read with great curiosity and absorption works on the blood and its circulation, a long step forward in understanding how the human body functions. This substitution my father had found would provide the life-supporting system, the removal of the waste products, the intake of oxygen through breathing, and so on. One thing was now clear to me, however: if this fluid was in fact what had coursed through the veins of the Monster, it was not restored through the human system of the body-manufacturing mechanism. No, it was more like filling a jar, say, with alcohol and sealing it. If for some reason the seal broke, it would in effect leak or even evaporate away. Or so it would seem, my mind stretching and almost creaking in new directions as I sought to comprehend the meaning of the fluid. How wise my aunt had been to bend my natural curiosity in directions toward the more conventional and practical role of a general physician, with a trained mind to follow the medical rules of the day in the treatment of the symptoms of disease and not to meddle with the natural processes of the universe. How unwise I had been to ignore this good advice and follow the perilous path of my father.

The words of Greene came back to me again. "I can only say this—for this is all I was told. The problem with the formula is that it is not viscous; it is too thin. This characteristic is attributed to the difference of chemicals in America or of water or both. In any case, it is hoped that you will be willing to experiment on this and produce not less than one gallon." Whatever was the root of the failure by those who had tried it in America, so it was with me.

I dined silently on cold roast beef and a bottle of Bordeaux, topped off with a slice of Camembert and a glass of port. The candles were dim and flickered from the April drafts that penetrated the windowpanes. William stood in his accustomed place three paces behind my chair, hearing every sigh as my mind remained fixed on the liquid in the laboratory. There were still a few days before Greene would return. In the meantime, I would retire again to the cellar and see if the passage of another twelve hours had wrought the necessary miracle.

The laboratory equipment remained as it was. If

William had been down snooping about on his master, there was no evidence. Yet I had the feeling that someone had been there—a smell, a turn of a flask as I picked it up. I put down my lamp and lighted the candles, and things were again as they had been the night before. I raised the flask with trembling hands and held it before the candle, as a wine connoisseur does a vintage bottle. It was as clear as before, but as thin and runny as a bad Beaujolais. I reviewed the formula in elaborate detail. Surely there was something I had ignored. I resolved to go through the whole process again, checking and re-checking each step. I placed the decanter on the edge of the bench by the candle, admiring again the rich color of the fluid, and busied myself with this unnatural work.

I weighed and measured with the precision of a pharmacist, heated each ingredient the precise amount, checked temperatures of the various small flasks, and then, after five hours, blended the whole mixture. There was again the puff of smoke and a smell of sulphur and formaldehyde, and the cloudy substance was on its slow path to clearing. It was at that moment viscous, and this time I thought I must have done it properly. I slumped into my chair and, powerless to help myself, fell into a deep and bottomless sleep. Again I had horrible dreams about the Fiend through a blur, never coming close enough for me to make him out, but most certainly there as a shadow in the night, an artificial voice of hate and threat, of consolation and sympathy, a tossing of a ship at sea, the roar of water, the flash of lightning. The smell of rotting flesh. This was what brought me up short. The sky was light gray. It was already past eight o'clock. The candles were almost gutted again. I seized the flask and held it to the window. The purple color was there, it was crystal clear and—and again, it was too thin. Too thin. I smashed the flask on the floor and watched the fluid trickle along the bricks as it found its way, like a series of snakes, toward the drain hole and disappeared. The nauseating odor remained, like the smell of a charnel house. I returned to my chair, dejected. More than dejected—my hands gripped the arms of the chair until my knuckles were white. I looked at my hands as though they belonged to someone else and were bent on their own destruction. Finally I arose and began to snuff out the dregs of candles with the silver spoon I had used to mix the formula. As I lowered it to a candle and, for some reason, held it there for a few seconds, I saw the drops left in the spoon visibly change to a darker and thicker hue. And then I looked at the first formula. Close to the candle, it too had changed in color and consistency. It might just do.

If there was an answer to the problem of the formula, it appeared to be reheating it, as a cook twice fries a potato to produce a *pomme fritte*. But why? Had my father thought that such a simple ruse as omitting this step in his formula might prevent someone who found his notebooks from repeating the experiment successfully? Possibly. There was no doubt it was now thicker, as though someone had poured a small amount of cornstarch into a sauce. Perhaps the additional time had done it on its own account, and the flame had played no role at all. So I would have to experiment with the fluid again and again. My copy of the formula was safely in my office, in my personal cabinet. I could work on several variations later. Right now I would make the required amount and reheat it and hope for the best. Whether the viscosity was permanent or would break down again under heat or cold was an open question, but that would have to be answered later.

As I continued to look through the flask into the candle, I was struck by another terrifying thought. It was as though the intensity of this labor and its association with my nightmares had unhinged my mind. Why should I help with this project? What evil might result? I would avoid the temptations of my father, which had carried him to a tragic end. Instead, I would satisfy the misgivings that now clouded my eyes. I would use the fluid itself as the means of my revenge. The idea was no sooner at hand than I acted on it. It was almost a matter of mean instinct, based on no moral philosophy, an act without a conscience. Into the flask I slowly tapped a powder of arsenic. It blended in without a trace.

On Friday the weather was again cold and sullen, and gusts of rain splashed on the French windows of the library. I was once again before the fire, pretending to read Harvey's *The Circulation of the Blood,* but, in truth, simply waiting for Greene. William was also anticipating his arrival. Uneasy he appeared, for perhaps he sensed, like a dog, that there was something wrong with Greene. I too would have been uneasy about him even if he had not been here on bizarre business. He came on time, like midnight, and there was nothing one could do about him, no more than stopping the wind or dispelling the fog.

His costume had not changed, as though he had spent his last week as a mannequin. The gold watch chain sagged across his waistcoat. His boots were muddy still, but that did not seem to bother him as it did William.

The formalities were almost identical with the previous visit, and we performed our parts in a mechanical fashion. There was no stirring of mutual animation that could lead to friendship. We were both all business, and after William had brought the silver tray with glasses and sherry and had retired (probably within earshot) the matter at hand rose like a jinni.

"What kind of success did you have?" asked Greene with his mechanical smile. His eyes had the same squirrel brightness, and his wispy reddish hair hung down his forehead like a wig. I hesitated. A look of fear spread over his eyes as though he were preparing to hear my failure or my refusal.

"Considerable," I said, and handed him from my inner jacket pocket a test tube, well stoppered. He eyed it with close curiosity and held it to the light of the fire. He shook it lightly. "It has a good consistency. I could not believe that there could be a difference in the chemicals, but indeed that must have been the case. Or was it the water? Or indeed the chemist? You have done it! How would you account for it?"

"First of all, we cannot jump to conclusions. It might not work, and it might not hold up. I can give you no advice on that."

He opened the test tube, smelled it, and rubbed a drop between his fingers. "I believe you have accomplished the task."

"But how, my dear Greene, can you say that?"

He smiled again, but there was no change in his countenance beyond that, and he did not respond.

I tried to draw him out and learn more about his

business in Baltimore, but his replies were evasive. A chandler does all kinds of things, and he was simply ordering more wares. Who had asked him to see me? He would not really explain, beyond his "friends." I could not believe that he did not know a good deal more than he was willing to reveal. Someone was trying the experiment and I, the son of Frankenstein, had been approached for help, although Greene never appealed to my rightful name. The gallon of liquid was in the hall closet, tightly stoppered in a wine jug. I could still refuse to give it to him or dash it to the floor, thereby disassociating myself from this curse. Or I could go under false colors, foiling the suspected user through the arsenic. I would hear of the failure from Greene and only then decide what I might do. I shuddered at my raw uncontrollable instinct, standing in the shade of one part of my personality.

"I must be on my way. I sail tonight. If you will provide me with the fluid . . ."

"I'll turn it over as we part."

With a certain banter unnatural to us both, we walked through the drawing room and into the marble hall, where William was already on hand with Mr. Greene's greatcoat and the wide-brimmed hat. As an afterthought, or so I tried to make it seem, I walked to the closet, picked up the jug, and walked with it toward Greene. "I'd like to provide a gift for your client. I doubt if you have Madeira like this in Baltimore."

"You are too kind," replied Greene, his eyes lighting up again. The jug was heavy and my palms were sweaty. To allow it to slip, dash it on the black-and-white tiled marble floor, was close to the connecting cells of my brain.

But before the crisis was reached, Greene took it from me and disappeared through the door that William held open.

"What manner of man is that?" William asked in amazement, in an expression of awe, suspicion, and yes, respect, but in an accusatory way, as though I knew the answer.

After Greene departed, up the drive came the carriage, swaying gently, with its lamps shining brightly in the drizzle. The horses stopped, the footman jumped to the door, and Aunt Margaret, fatigued and rumpled, eased out of the carriage. And just behind was the loveliest girl that I had ever seen.

CHAPTER III

KIDNAPED

"VICTOR, VICTOR," was the sound that awoke me from wild dreams of tossing at sea, in vain attempts to cast overboard casks of wine that were boiling at the calking. An angel with golden hair hovered over the bow.

"Victor," Aunt Margaret said, "I must tell you of the past week, so you will know about Felicia's situation." In not too many words, she covered a very tragic story. The Reverend John McInnes and his wife, Sarah, had both succumbed to cholera, victims of their humanitarian efforts to aid the afflicted. Felicia in turn had cared for them in their hour of suffering, as had my aunt, and through a kind of miracle, an intervention of fate for whatever reason, Felicia and Aunt Margaret were both spared. Both Mr. McInnes and his wife died horrible deaths. An only child, Felicia had now only the support of Aunt Margaret. "But it is no solution for me to keep her here. Her father's brother is also an Evangelical minister and he has a parish in Washington, in America. I must write to him immediately and make the arrangements. In the meantime, Felicia is our guest and will be treated as a member of the family." To my knowledge, this was the first dissenter we had had inside the house.

She was not down for breakfast, so I relied for the moment on our hurried meeting of the previous evening to keep her beauty fresh in my mind's eye. She was no taller than my shoulder, lithe and small boned. She had ringlets and curls of golden hair, wide-set eyes of China blue, a perfect nose. Her cheekbones were high and her lips full in a slightly pouting manner. She was as light as I was dark.

I was not disappointed at our second meeting. If anything, she was more beautiful, more charming. She moved with the grace of a wild animal. For almost two weeks we all went on a discreet round of quiet entertainment, the theater, sight-seeing and the like, taking advantage of the improving weather. All this helped alleviate the gloom of her tragedy and seemed also to improve my own outlook. My headaches, for example, disappeared. I was so caught up in her beauty and charm that I had difficulty thinking about myself. Yet my infrequent misery showed, so that one evening at the end of April she asked me directly what was troubling me. We were alone in the library, the fireplace still bright and cheery, a last fire of spring. We had port, and Aunt Margaret had already made her way to her chambers.

Felicia was staring into the fire. I observed her lips closely, noting a hint of sensuality there that was scarcely concealed behind the mourning and proper manners. The fire and wine were relaxing her, and she was coming out of the unnatural state into which she had been cast.

She looked around the room and began to admire some jade pieces displayed on one shelf of the bookcase.

"Your aunt has some splendid pieces of jade."

"Compliments of Captain Walton's travels in the Orient."

"Which one do you like the best?"

"I think the bird."

"The phoenix."

"Is that what it is?" I asked.

"Yes, it is a spirit that rises from the ashes."

"And which is your favorite?" I asked.

"I think I like best the ink pot."

"You noticed the bat and the peach leaves."

"What does that represent?" she asked.

"Longevity."

She eyed it more closely. "I see it is slightly cracked. A hairline fracture."

"I know," I said.

Then she turned from the jade and focused on me. "You are troubled tonight, Victor. If there is anything you want to tell me, please do."

I shook my head, but then, to my surprise, I began to tell her the story of my father in detail, seeing before my eyes the pages of Captain Walton's letters. It was as though the pages were bound in my brain and were turned at just the right moment by the blink of her eyes, wide with amazement, horror, disbelief, compassion. As I talked, my spirits rose and the terrible grip about my forehead loosened. Her clear eyes clouded at the end of my story, and we both wept. The clock sounded a single stroke, bringing us back from the icy north.

"Oh, Victor, it is a beautiful, tragic tale. My heart goes out to you."

Then the fireplace surged from a down draft of wet April wind, and the sound of the great clock in the hall accented the momentary silence between us.

"You can understand now," I said evenly, "why my aunt insisted that I eschew the name of Frankenstein and why I face the world as Victor Saville."

"Not completely, dear Victor. The curse has passed, and it is a loss to the world that such an accomplishment should receive no notice. Think of the good that could have come of such knowledge."

"That's true," I replied, not suggesting that this very thought for too long had sustained my imagination and longings and was on its way, despite my best desires, to claiming yet another victim. "But even if the work could somehow be reconstructed, what of the temptation, the corruption that might arise?"

"That's why it is a pity that in some way that power cannot pass to you. For you know full well the dangers and could act accordingly to see that there was no misuse of this extraordinary gift."

"You think the morality, the ethics of the matter are that simple?" I asked.

"You mean the question of creation itself?" She paused. "I come from a Christian background, and the fact of divine creation is accepted without argument. But if this Monster was animated as you describe, does not the hand of the Creator have to be involved; otherwise, wouldn't it be impossible?"

I lowered my eyes. "I don't know. I really don't." Our eyes caught for a moment, but with an intensity that

I had never experienced. Her breathing was quick. My obsession with the creative process centered in her small frame. We both rose, and I took her hand. We walked quietly, slowly through the great hall and up the circular staircase. At the landing we kissed briefly, but hungrily. And she went off to her quarters, and I went slowly, confusedly, off to mine.

That night the pain returned to my brain with a vengeance. The next day I was drained of energy and sensibility, as though a great vampire, the size of an Asian fruit bat, had infiltrated my bedroom and sucked at the sources of my system, my sanity, and my soul. William hovered around like a hummingbird, always there prying —always prying with his supercilious obedience. "Will that be all, sir?" provoking me to say, "Yes, I need nothing. Nothing at all." Felicia appeared, but only briefly and vaguely and always in the company of my aunt. My thoughts of Felicia were blocked by the question of what had happened to the liquid I delivered to Greene. Were these fiendish pains the Devil's revenge for my wild guess of the possible recipient? My conscience was deeply troubled, and I regretted that my unconsidered continuation of my father's battle, if that was what it was, had gotten off to a wretched start. My best and clearest thinking seemed to arise immediately after the event was already in train.

Then after perhaps two weeks, in a brief moment in the afternoon, the sun appeared as though it belonged to a different solar system, huge and bright and hot, and all the miasmata of the winter were burned away in the great blast of the sun's furnace. The world was suddenly bright again, and in the day's mail, delivered on a silver tray by William, there was a letter in a large envelope, with my name written as though it were engraved. The return address was from F. Greene, Importers. It lay on my breakfast tray like an invitation.

Dear Dr. Saville, I am pleased to say that our recent transaction was successful from all points of view. You have in fact given great impetus to our research project—so much so that my colleagues and I would like you to join forces with us and participate as a partner in several ventures well within your area of competence. To solidify our co-operation, however, it will be necessary for you to visit our main office here so that you will be able to judge the potential for yourself. Our company would be pleased to arrange for your transportation and any expenditures related to your visit. I would hope you will respond favorably and be able to arrive by early June. Your obedient servant, F. Greene.

I regarded the letter with a gradually clearing head and ambivalent feelings. I knew that the formula was flawed, yet Greene stated that it was "successful from all points of view." Instead of suggesting that I manufacture more, he wrote, "It will be necessary for you to visit our main office." This would place me in their power if this scheme, as I had now to assume, was experimentation in my father's pioneer work in the creation of human life. I hesitated. Would it not be wise to feel out the situation from the safety of London? Rising from my bed and walking unsteadily to my desk, I wrote Greene to that effect; that is, that he should visit me in London and give me a more precise notion of what was wanted, how much time might be involved, and so forth before I could consider my situation and advise him one way or the other. I rang for William and bade him to post my letter.

My health quickly improved—especially my mental outlook, for no sooner was I back in the daily company of Felicia than the thoughts of Greene vanished, and my mind filled with dreams of romance in the delights of the garden and the blossoms, the aroma of the boxwood, and the cool, sweet smell of the grass.

"Victor, life is so pleasant here that I could stay on forever."

"And why not?"

"My uncle wrote, and I have booked passage in just one week."

My face grayed like a winter's day, and she was touched. "We'll write to each other, Victor, and heaven knows, we may meet again some time." The arch of her eyebrows and the quick laugh indicated depths of personality and a feeling for innuendo that I had not previously detected in our limited and proper friendship. She leaned gently and wickedly against my shoulder, and I blushed at the cleavage of her breasts and the cool of her hand on mine. But in a second she was on her feet, swinging her bonnet and shaking her long golden hair, absorbing the sun in a very un-British way.

I made no response, but realized that there was a deadline facing me; that is, whatever relationship was established within that period of time would govern it for however long it might endure.

William remained as solicitous as ever, though he had

taken on the additional chore of arranging for Felicia's departure. He had not spoken of Greene since the latter left, nor did I, concluding that there was nothing to be gained in mentioning that macabre fellow. Yet he was on my mind now again, a good deal, and on the few occasions when I returned to my laboratory and William came by, I could feel that he had made the connection that Greene was related to my experimentation. Instead, he spoke movingly of Felicia's tragedy, in much more detail than I knew, and the pity of her going off to America—a strange land, and a stranger there herself.

"I have seldom seen a more comely lass, Doctor, or one of such general good humor."

"I share your high regard for Miss McInnes," I replied, "but Aunt Margaret believes that she should be with her own blood. And you know that Aunt Margaret is generally correct, specializing as she does in bringing in waifs from the cold and teaching them what is right."

William's look did not please me, and I felt a sudden flush of anger (or was it jealousy?) that William was taking such liberties above his station. He was not insensitive to my change in manner and limped off, leaving me to my halfhearted analysis of blood samples and to my own brooding. I wondered what Aunt Margaret really thought about Felicia, not as a temporary ward, but in relation to me. She would not be likely to approve of Felicia, her being Evangelical and without means, two characteristics that often went together. On the other hand, she was charmed by her manner and beauty. And she would modify her view one way or the other, I should imagine, depending on my own desires and intentions. There, indeed, was the rub. My desires were clear enough, but my intentions? I was still a Frankenstein, fated to be caught up in the cycle started by my father. Had it not already happened, with no wish, no desire on my part? Could I really ask anyone to share this responsibility that I might not fulfill any more successfully than had my father? Was this the reason for my hesitancy to speak more openly and frankly with her about the thoughts that had risen to the very tip of my tongue and had then fallen back, like an exhausted mountaineer, no more to challenge the summit of my aspirations in her regard?

The evenings were longer and longer, and the June air was pleasant after dinner. I took with me two glasses of port, and we sat in the garden on a long stone bench. There were bats flitting through the air, and the twilight hung lovingly like a tender kiss.

"The time is running down, Felicia, and there are some things we must discuss."

"Oh, really," she replied, smiling but mocking my tardy speech.

"It is the Frankenstein shadow that envelops my soul and obscures the happiness I would gladly seek."

"You make too much of the past, Victor. You've allowed yourself to be closed into a tiny room by the evidence of the past. It is not locked, Victor—the door is not locked—and for you to leave and go on to other chambers, all you have to do is to will it."

"If I could only agree with that. If I only could." I then related, in sparse terms, my encounter with Greene, omitting the arsenic and the letter requesting my presence. This statement had a sombering effect on her, and she looked at me with concern. She fitted easily into the hollow of my shoulder, and we sat silent for minutes, like children comforting each other after the loss of a favorite pet. "And so that is what causes that faraway look, Victor, and not, as I had thought, someone else who might deserve your thoughts more than I."

I held her even more tightly, and there were more moments of silence as the darkening scene took hold of us. "I'm not afraid, Victor. I know you are strong and some-how will manage." We kissed gently but seriously, as though savoring that particular moment beyond any other. Almost as in a dream we were on the damp grass in front of the bench. She sobbed, "I am yours, Victor, body and soul."

I kissed her eyes and felt a moment of electric excite-ment. "I love you, Felicia," I said, but I was unable to go on further and talk of matrimony.

The great blinding headache struck like an arrow, and the dignity of our return into the drawing room through the French windows was marred by my clutching my head and Felicia's worrying over her gown, brushing off bits of twigs and grass. We embraced again on the stairs and she hurried off toward her quarters and I to my pleasant chambers. What I had fantasized for so many days was in one brief moment history. I suspected that she had thought considerably about the subject too, and for both of us to have been overcome in such an unlikely circum-stance, in one grand moment of passion, left a bittersweet sensation. With the excitement gone, there was a sense of shame, as though this deeper commitment to a more com-plex relationship were simply meaningless.

My head cleared almost as quickly as the pain had come, and my thoughts were calmer but no more satisfactory. She would share my stained and endangered name, of that I was certain. The question remained, did I want her to share it . . . or, in fact, anyone? Put differently, was it a burden that could be borne only by me, like Christ and his cross? I slept uncertainly during the night, and then, with the perverseness of nature, around 5 A.M. fell into a sleep of the just. I awoke greatly refreshed and with an untroubled mind, but only for a moment. On my breakfast tray was a note from my aunt. While it was not unprecedented for her to request my presence in the morning, it was unusual enough to cause concern. I dressed in fresh linen, breeches, and a lace-trimmed shirt. In the mirror I was the picture of confidence, with a bad conscience. This feeling persisted when I knocked on her door and entered the bright sitting room. It intensified when I looked out the window and slightly to my left. The stone bench in the garden was clearly visible. But not Aunt Margaret. She was still in her darkened bedroom.

"Victor," she sobbed from her pillow, "I have failed you. I have brought temptation into this house. I've ruined you with this scheming Jezebel. You too must repent, Victor, or spend eternity in hell."

"Pull the shade," she commanded. And when I did her bidding, she raised her bedside Bible, placed her glasses at the exact calibration on her nose, and read, " 'Behold, I will cast her into a bed, and them that commit adultery with her into great tribulation, except they repent of their deeds.' "

For reply I was silent.

"Victor, this girl is evil. She was passed over by the illness that claimed her parents for the work of the Devil. She will destroy you. Have no more to do with her."

"She leaves tomorrow. . . ."

"See that she does, and then let peace and tranquillity reign again. I set out to do the Lord's work and look what it's gotten me."

"I'm truly sorry. I don't know what else I can say. But I do ask your forgiveness."

"It's the Lord's forgiveness you should seek."

I returned to my room to contemplate this disaster. In hindsight I now realized she had had reservations about Felicia all along as she took her from one place to another in the city at a pace designed, in retrospect, to minimize our intimate association.

It was Sunday. At breakfast I made excuses for my aunt and suggested that we go ahead with the plans for church. Contrite in the closed carriage, I apprised Felicia of my aunt's intelligence.

"I'm sorry, Victor, then, for her sake. But more important to me, Victor, is how do you feel about all this? About me? About us?"

I smiled and squeezed her hand gently. "Aunt Margaret thinks you are Jezebel."

During the service I noticed Felicia leafing through her Bible. Then she handed it to me. The book was the last—Revelation.

"Notwithstanding I have a few things against thee, because thou sufferest that woman Jezebel, which calleth herself a prophetess, to teach and to seduce my servants to commit fornication, and to eat things sacrificed unto idols. And I gave her space to repent of her fornication; and she repented not."

She raised her pure, clear eyes and looked deeply into mine until I felt weak. "Do you think I have the power of prophecy?"

I made no answer, as though silence would resolve the issue that hung over us like a rain-filled cloud.

"The future," she said at length, "is a little clearer now than it was."

The return in the carriage heightened the tension. Each time I tried to form a phrase, it tangled on my tongue. Felicia was silent, and I feared she might soon burst out crying. "We'll have some time after luncheon, darling," I ventured. "What would you prefer to do?"

"Oh, Victor. How little we know each other. We met as strangers, and now we part as strangers."

"That's not so at all. You are my closest friend. I've shared intimacies with you that I've shared with no other."

Now she seemed preoccupied. She soon looked up and seemed to see me as a new person, someone of interest. "I know, Victor, let's look at Captain Walton's letters. I must know them better, if I am to know you at all."

The weather was clouding over and, having no better suggestion, I welcomed a way to spend these awkward hours—awkward because I was as undecided about myself as I was about Felicia. Upon learning from William that Aunt Margaret continued to be indisposed, we dispensed with a formal luncheon, snacked on bread and meat, and went directly to my quarters. The rooms were always bright, with three high windows on either outer wall. In addition to the canopied bed, there were my tall desk and two comfortable chairs. I removed the packet of letters from the lower drawer of the desk. We chose, instinctively, the floor, the Oriental carpet next to my bed, and as I lay on my back, trying to relax, Felicia began going through the letters, here swiftly, there slowly, gathering the mood of the letters and the dreariness of the day. After some time, she shook me gently.

"Victor, listen to this. 'It was already one in the morning; the rain pattered dismally against the panes, and my candle was nearly burnt out, when, by the glimmer of the half-extinguished light, I saw the dull yellow eye of the creature open; it breathed hard, and a convulsive motion agitated its limbs.

" 'How can I describe my emotions at this catastrophe, or how delineate the wretch whom with such infinite pains and care I had endeavoured to form? His limbs were in proportion, and I had selected his features as beautiful. Beautiful!—Great God! His yellow skin scarcely covered the work of muscles and arteries beneath; his hair was a lustrous black, and flowing; his teeth of a pearly whiteness; but these luxuriances only formed a more horrid contrast with his watery eyes, that seemed almost of the same colour as the dun white sockets in which they were set, his shrivelled complexion and straight black lips.' "

The image rose before my closed eyes, and I could see my horror-struck father flee into the night from the clutch of his creation.

"How I marvel at this tale," said Felicia. "How I marvel that it's true. Were it not for you and these letters to vouch for it, I fear I would doubt it altogether."

"When I think of the tragedy of it all, I become morose, depressed, call it what you will. You can see, I think, how I, the survivor, am still victimized by that hallucination, that creation. I fear it accounts for my confusion, my hesitation to impose my love and my burden on you."

"I wonder, Victor, if anyone can help in that regard." She continued to leaf through more letters.

"The name, then, of Frankenstein does not raise in you the fear that it has for my aunt, for example?" I waited anxiously for her reply.

"No, Victor. Nor does the tale of the Monster himself. Take this passage of the Monster, for example. It's beautiful. 'Oh, Frankenstein, be not equitable to every other, and trample upon me alone, to whom thy justice, and even thy clemency and affection, is most due. Remember, that I am thy creature; I ought to be thy Adam; but I am rather the fallen angel, whom thou drivest from joy for no misdeed. Everywhere I see bliss, from which I alone am irrevocably excluded. I was benevolent and good; misery made me a fiend. Make me happy, and I shall again be virtuous.' "

With that she sobbed long sobs, and fell upon my chest convulsively. I placed my arms around her, and we lay in the gathering gloom, both weeping—we knew not for whom, and neither asked. After a while, she shook herself free and quickly went on to the end, already knowing the story as I had told it. Finally, she put down the letters, profoundly moved—and puzzled. Her bright, quick face was furrowed and troubled. "The creator and his creature. Both died of horrible unhappiness. Do people still die of unhappiness, Victor?"

"What really killed my father?" I said. "He could have turned back at any time from his pursuit of the

Monster. Yet he went on to a certain death, alone. Was this a kind of expiation?"

"The moral question of ultimate responsibility. Does this sin, if such it was, pass from father to son?" she asked.

"Sin? Disease? Since the visit of Mr. Greene from Baltimore I've known little peace. Had you not been here, God alone knows what would have happened to me."

She looked away, and I feared that I had offended her by revealing that my new-found love was merely a diversion from this obsession. "The evidence that the results of my father's experimentation are in someone's hand is quite clear. To find out who has those notebooks, who is involved, addles my brain and sours my more pleasant thoughts. Can you see why I'm so unsatisfactory in my affair of the heart?"

"If the information exists," she said, "you would tempt the same fate. Although as I have said, having suffered, you would avoid the evil. But, as I speak these words, is that possible?"

"I'm an indifferent student of the Bible. But I recall no prohibition, from Moses on, that 'Thou shalt not create.' "

"I'll review the theology of this with my uncle in America and send you a letter with a full explanation."

This simple statement brought us both abruptly back to the reality of her departure, but strangely settled our mood and disposition. I had never felt closer to anyone in my life, and I knew that our destinies were intertwined. She seemed to sense the same thought, and there was a tranquillity over her countenance, an extra aura of beauty, that had lately been missing. We kissed briefly, and she left the room. I gently returned the letters to the lower drawer. They had earned their repose.

The departure before dawn, in the rain, proceeded like the final act of a play. The plot set in motion, the actors go on to the end, whatever roles they have. Felicia's great ship trunk was strapped to the rear of the carriage, and William rode alongside the coachman through the fog toward the Thames wharf where the American ship, the *Blue Dolphin,* would leave on the six o'clock tide. Felicia and I were in the closed carriage, my heart pounding, for the imminence of her departure had yet failed to crystallize my plans.

"Darling, what am I to say that I can vouchsafe and you can accept while I resolve my business with Mr. Greene?"

"If you are asking my advice, I would say to avoid him, refrain from becoming involved in any way whatever with the enterprise, no matter how innocently. I know for myself that the letters strangely excited me, but I know it is evil. Not like the pleasures of the flesh, the evil of Jezebel. No. This is a subtler corruption, Victor, one that I do not know how to describe. My late dear father could. The end of such a fascination is simply unpredictable. That aside and forgotten, Victor, we could . . ."

I held her in my arms. She was right, of course, yet I could not say the words to unite our fate, to break with the past. I could feel her embrace begin to relax when those vows were not forthcoming, as though she realized that no one, however lovely, could yet cope with my obsession.

"I wish you well, Victor," she said. "I fear for you,

and I'll pray for you—if prayers from such a sinner as me are of value to heaven."

The carriage had now reached the dock. There was the bustle of stevedores completing the loading of cargo—cotton goods, cutlery, china. It would still be some time before the ship sailed. William oversaw the carrying off of the trunk and small cases, and Felicia and I walked slowly, silently, arm in arm, toward the *Blue Dolphin*, whose rigging was now visible through the morning mist and fog, which excluded anything beyond our immediate view. I was trying to compose myself for an appropriate farewell, one that would not cut my ties with this lovely girl but would not, on the other hand, commit me inexorably to matrimony. I guided her behind a pile of cargo boxes. As I placed my arms around her, I was conscious of the strong odor of chloroform and a mind-numbing blow to the head.

CHAPTER IV

BERKELEY SPRINGS

THE JARRING OF A WAGON shook the final cobwebs from my mind. A gag was in my mouth, and I was tied, trussed like a pheasant. I had experienced variations of this condition during the entire crossing of the Atlantic, broken only by short periods of release when I was given small amounts of food and drink and an opportunity to relieve my churning bowels. I had apparently been smuggled aboard and had been kept from the sight of the crew. My captor and tormentor had been Greene himself. No one else had appeared. He had been as uncommunicative as the tomb. His odd features had assumed a frightful cast, and I had comforted myself during the tossing of the ship with daydreams of dissecting him joint by joint.

That and the thought of Felicia, whose whereabouts were not known to me, had maintained my determination. Greene would not respond to my repeated queries. Had I only been bolder, declared my honest intentions and made her my wife in London, perhaps this nightmare would not have started. Ah, if only I knew my honest intentions. My preoccupation with the Monster had already subverted my best chance for love. If there were not room for both, then I must choose love. If I extricated myself from this horror, and if I again found Felicia, who danced in my brain like a golden sunbeam, I would devote my life to her.

I had never anticipated that my dealing with Greene would come to this pass. All I had done was to produce the fluid, indeed a seminal work. But what of the fluid itself? Had it been used? What had the results been? Surely the arsenic poison in it would kill a sensate being. Only something with arteries of copper or glass could survive such a concoction. Yet Greene's letter had been quite specific that the sample was satisfactory. His attitude toward me was peculiar, however—controlled rage that strained his singular features to the utmost. What did he want of me? He simply refused to answer during our daily encounters in the pitlike cell where I was held. Yet I had no real sense of fear at this juncture. Greene would not take the trouble to transport me for the simple pleasure of strangling me in that hole or slipping me over the rail. Hardly that. Yet it pained him to have any dealing with me. Therefore, he was acting under a powerful compulsion that for the moment overcame his revulsion toward me.

Until I was deposited in the wagon, I had retained the hope that I would somehow be rescued at sea or, barring that, that once the ship entered a harbor, the authorities of the realm would assert themselves. People of my kind simply did not disappear. And what of poor William? Crippled, how would he stand against the assault on the London wharf? Had he been seized, or had he escaped in the fog? Perhaps gimpy old William had escaped the assault and had alerted the authorities. But hope no longer sustained me as I looked toward a high-vaulted and blue heaven and onto a lower vista, the crates and boxes and an alert German shepherd dog that shared the wagon with me.

My mind again played on Felicia. My heart ached. In her innocence she had become involved in this ugly scene —saved from the evils of poverty and misuse by my aunt's generous intervention only to be caught up in the curious web of the son of Frankenstein. I longed to hold her, to reassure her that all was well, that I loved her as no one could love anyone else. A child of love and hope, she was slighted through no fault of her own in this desperate scheme of unprincipled men—and I alone was responsible.

And where was aid and succor? As for myself, I had been removed from the ship in a packing crate. Did no one know where I was? Aunt Margaret surely would have moved the authorities to do their duty. All I had at the moment for a certitude was myself, which was neither comforting nor reassuring. How could I prevail, or even survive, against these forces of evil, now surely in command?

The horses were rested at intervals, and I could hear the murmur of conversation from the two men on the buckboard. A third man followed the wagon on horseback. The easy canter sounded clear above the rattle of the metal wheels on the stony road. As I was jostled about, the pain in my head transferred to my ankles and wrists, like electricity being conducted down a wire. The rope was wearing into my wrists and, despite the strength of a surgeon's hands, I could not twist them loose. I was also preoccupied over possibly losing control of my bladder and anal sphincter. The very thought of beshatting myself, however, tightened the process; and I remained tied, but clean, on the bottom of the rumbling wagon. The growing heat sent rivulets of sweat down my face and back. I entered into a torpor, a state of nonidentification with the quick or the dead, and in this way survived another day.

Finally, it was dark and the wagon again halted. After a delay, the blanket was thrown off me, the ropes were released simultaneously from my hands and feet, and the gag was taken from my mouth. There was a pause, then, "We will stay here for the night, Frankenstein. You can remove yourself from the wagon for food." The voice was cold and flat, yet it represented the one single strand of continuity in this bizarre affair—the person of Frederick Greene. His round hat was dusty. His features, which had only seemed odd in the safety of Aunt Margaret's library, looked sinister in the light of heaven and the flickering of a new campfire.

I sat up with difficulty, and my groans were audible.

"Do not pity yourself excessively," said Greene. "This has been a matter of inconvenience for all parties. But there was nothing else to do after you declined our urgent invitation."

My temper flared. "Violating the law, seizing my person—all this must be accounted for in good time. Now, what of the girl, the young lady I was taking to the ship?"

"She has not been harmed," said Greene.

"But where is she?" I insisted.

Greene smiled his crooked smile. "She is in good hands."

My feeling of discomfiture was giving way to anger.

I got off the wagon and stood unsteadily. "And what of William?"

"These matters will eventually be clear," Greene replied tartly and turned to rejoin his two companions at the campfire a short distance away.

I reached out my left hand and grabbed him by the shoulder. "I want to know right now, you wretch. I . . ."

Greene turned toward me and with one powerful backhanded blow smashed me to the ground. The dog grabbed my arm as I reached for Greene, and Greene began kicking me and cursing over my prostrate body. I protected my head and vital parts as best I could. Blood poured from my nose and a cut on my lip. Then suddenly there was an intervention.

"Greene, in the name of God, let the man be."

The kicking ceased as Greene turned toward the intervener. "This has nothing to do with the work of the Lord or the Devil, Ritter. I'll have none of your drunken interference."

"Have a care, Greene. Do not press me too far. I am more vital to the success of this enterprise than you, by far."

The man facing Greene was of the cloth. He was slightly built, with a dark, thin face. Yet before the stare and threat of Greene, Ritter began to lose ground. As he backed away, he bowed his head and sobs wracked his body. He turned and walked toward the trees.

As I still lay on the ground in great pain, Greene glared at me and in a hissing tone cursed me again. My ears rang and, startled and weak from the loss of blood, I did nothing. Greene's eyes glowed. There was a meanness

—or madness?—in his twisted look, but his anger had drained away. He spoke to the dog, which released its grip and bounded away. I went on my hands and knees toward the nearest tree and, reaching it, leaned heavily against it. The earth turned as my spinning head fought a feeling of many-colored dizziness.

"Take this," said the voice of the minister. He had come to me silently from the dark. He brought the blanket from the wagon and a tin cup of water and a cloth. He wiped the blood from my face and used the cloth as a compress over my nose and lip. I drank greedily, and the water flowed into my system as if I were a sponge.

"Take care not to arouse Greene's ire," said Ritter softly. "He loses control easily and appears at times not to be responsible for his actions, either in deed or word."

The heavy smell of alcohol confirmed Greene's accusation. From the light of the fire I could see the redness of Ritter's eyes and the stubble of his dark beard. Still here was my first potential ally in this mad scene, and I was grateful for his assistance.

"Ritter," came the call from Greene, "let him be."

Ritter gave my arm a comforting squeeze but responded quickly to Greene's command. As Ritter departed, toward me came the driver of the wagon, a grotesque, misshapen man, stunted from the waist up. He too wore a large gray hat, but of triangular design, which gave him a dramatic macabre appearance. His face was bland, his eyes watery, and his teeth too small and too even. He placed a cup of hot soup beside me and handed me a substantial chunk of bread. The legs went away, the body appearing to be on a walking tray, so incongruous was

their size. The hat bobbed in step as though it were inde-
pendently suspended from an invisible cord. I ate slowly,
chewing the bread thoroughly and savoring the vegetable
soup. My mind clung to those two things—the bread and
the soup—as a needed respite from the constantly unhappy
thoughts which had filled my brain since the fateful morning on the wharf.

The long shadow of Greene fell over my face, and I
looked up with apprehension. "I need not emphasize that
you are here at my pleasure and that your co-operation
fully given is your best pledge for returning safely to your
home. Otherwise, I will make no guarantee about your
fate."

"So it is yours to determine?"

Greene shrugged. "You should perform on that
premise."

A rush of questions welled up in my mind. What
guarantee for safety did I in fact have, in view of Greene's
contempt and the Monster's hatred of my father? What
in the end did they want me to do? Was I to assist in some
unholy experiment, or worse—and this idea had been with
me for a week, like a maggot in a wound—was I to be included in the experiment itself? Once they had mastered
the technique of making the fluid, which they might ex-
tort from me or someway learn, then of what value was I
to them? But no words formed on my thick tongue. There
was no need to risk provoking Green's wrath, which apparently knew no season or bounds. I would instead hold
myself in check, waiting for a more suitable and safer opportunity to pose these nagging inquiries.

"You do understand my meaning, Frankenstein,"

Greene continued. "I would prefer that whatever happens is not because of a misapprehension." The menace in his voice was black as night.

"I will do what I must," I replied enigmatically.

Greene seemed satisfied, however, with that answer and did not press me further. "There will be no need to bind you. I rely on your co-operation and the vigilance of the dog to assure us all a peaceful night."

I rubbed my arm instinctively where the animal's teeth had all but broken the skin. It crouched not ten feet away, its long tongue hanging between its glistening canine teeth, its ears and eyes alert for any untoward movement on my part. As Greene turned to leave, I tried to form another question, to clarify the situation before I was overwhelmed by speculation. "I am taken against my will. If my co-operation is wanted, should not more concern be shown about my own sensibilities in this matter? And should I not be consulted on the ultimate aim of any project, any scheme, involving my father's knowledge learned at what costs?" But again my muddled mind refused to function. Warmed by the blanket and partially restored by the food and water, I found to my relief that sleep was not elusive.

For the next three days I was allowed to sit in the rear of the wagon, unbound, but with the faithful German shepherd dog in his accustomed place. He responded to the name Prince. A prisoner still, I was at least able to view the countryside. There were cleared farms, but mostly trees, rising up and up toward the hazy and purpling mountains. Greene had even disclosed our destination, Berkeley Springs, Virginia. This meant nothing to me, yet it burned in my mind like Mecca. There would be an end to the journey. And from the signs at crossroads I judged we would be there that afternoon. My spirits rose and fell like the mountains and valleys, but I became more alert as the sense of foreboding came across me like the late afternoon breeze. I took stock of the supplies in the wagon—boxes and barrels of flour, salt, cloth, gunpowder, and perhaps weapons. I speculated as to whether they were simply for commercial purposes under Greene's aegis or for something more sinister.

The hours passed. In one pleasant valley I was struck by a passing group of farm children because of their sallow complexion, pointed features, and vacuous expression.

"Their appearance?" responded Greene, whose mood had also undergone a kind of metamorphosis for the better. He rocked on the buckboard before me and answered, "The result of too much inbreeding in the valley. The Hessian troops were mustered out in this area, and they stayed on—with their own kind."

The road was climbing slowly into higher elevations. In the near distance was a range of mountains, dominating the verdant valley. But no sooner had I begun to absorb the vista than there was a sign, "Berkeley Springs Inn. Meals. Sulphur baths." The inn was a pleasant collection of white buildings in the Colonial style. A sweeping roof and well-proportioned columns and a wide circular drive set apart the main building. The horses and the driver and Greene and Prince all seemed familiar with the environs as we drove straight down a side path to the furthest cottage. "You will stay here, Doctor, as will the dog."

I launched myself from the wagon and entered the

cottage as directed, the dog remaining outside on the porch. The idea of escape at this juncture was now far back in my mind. First, there was the high risk, but beyond that were my curiosity and apprehension. There was the sense that in this wild and rustic atmosphere was the key to creation, and I wanted to have it in my own pocket. I was drawn to the scene as iron filings are to a magnet.

The cottage was absolutely quiet. There was a pleasant sitting room with a fireplace and two closed rooms leading off from it. I tried the knob of the door to my left and entered. There by the bed was a trunk, precisely like one at Aunt Margaret's. Opened, it revealed a supply of my own apparel. And alongside the trunk was my black medical bag. Instead of reflecting on this phenomenon, I moved directly to the washbasin, depositing my filthy clothes and luxuriating as I washed my arms and face in the tepid water, which turned dark gray before my eyes. I bathed the remainder of my body as best I could with the limited facilities. My ablutions once completed, I changed into fresh linen and outfitted myself with a green jacket and brown trousers, which seemed suitable for this mountain retreat.

Enormously refreshed, I turned my attention to the contents of my medical case: a substantial quantity of pills, drugs, and palliatives; carbolic acid and a large bottle of alcohol; an oilskin. Then I felt behind the velvet lining and there, secure, was a single-shot pistol. I had long carried it against the possibility of trouble on my way to and from the hospital. Now I would simply leave it where it was. It was an ally of uncertain value, like the Reverend

Ritter. He had disappeared, incidentally, the same evening, going on ahead to whatever was his destination.

Pacing slowly back and forth, I made my way again into the sitting room. The door to the other room was closed, with a key in the lock. I opened it and entered. The shades were drawn against the late afternoon sun. There in the bed in the corner was someone asleep or resting. There was no acknowledgment of my entry and no sound as I moved closer, but soon the figure on the bed heard my approach and turned and looked up at me with a startled face. Not, however, as startled as mine.

"Victor. Oh, Victor!"

I drew Felicia to my breast and showered kisses on her lovely face. Her sobs of joy quickened my being. But the flowering of this moment was blighted by a heavy pounding on the door. There was no choice but to open it.

"William!" I exclaimed and extended my hand. The forces of good were reassembling and the prospects for a happy resolution soared. But my man of twenty years recoiled from my proffered greeting as though it were an odious reptile and stood stiffly beside Greene. "I think you labor under a false illusion about my present status in life. I am known here, Dr. Frankenstein, as Mr. Digby. Surnames are not the exclusive property of the rich."

Greene motioned for us to sit. "You and Digby can compose at some future date your personal differences, Frankenstein, for time is of the essence. You are to leave immediately for the mountains, where your work will begin. You will be escorted to the proper trail by Digby here. Digby must return to arrange for supplies. . . ."

And Greene caught himself, as though undecided what more to say. "We are shorthanded at the moment, but only for the moment, and at some places. There is no question of your considering any kind of escape, or doing anything that does not correspond to our wishes. If you and the lady are to resume your previous circumstances, then my point is self-evident. We are a responsible enterprise and we require discipline and full co-operation. Any lapse on your part, Frankenstein, will have repercussions for both of you."

"Why the haste?" I pleaded, desperate for time alone with Felicia to learn of her situation and any facts she might have discovered.

Greene's face clouded over like a Swiss mountain peak. His facial muscles twitched and there was the sense of barely controlled rage. "Suffice to say my interpretation of the need is all that is necessary."

"Sufficient unto the day is the evil thereof," I responded.

"Prepare your clothing and check your medical bag," said Greene in his cold, flat tone. "If there are any common supplies needed, let me know. The horses will be at the door in about ten minutes."

"But what of Felicia?"

"She is in our hands as an earnest of your sincerity. She will be along. Later."

Felicia assisted me in packing the saddlebags that William Digby had brought. Digby indeed. For twenty years the scoundrel had nourished himself in my aunt's home, all the while plotting against the very family that had salvaged him from the human garbage bin. He stood over us in a mocking manner, reducing our conversation to tatters of unrevealing phrases. That chore done, I rose and held Felicia in my arms, scowling sharply at William. Embarrassed, he retreated to the sitting room, still within general earshot but out of range of whispers and endearments.

"Victor, my blood runs cold with fear. There is a frightful affair involving the Monster. He lives. Lives of many people—a revolution, perhaps—are in the balance."

"Can you be more precise?"

"I have overheard some things, but no, not really." Sobs completed her response.

I calmed her brow with my kisses, but I too was in a state of high agitation. I had kept my mind, my deepest thoughts, away from the truth of the situation—that the Fiend himself was high in those brooding mountains. He wanted me—for no good. And he had me effectively in his power. There was no escape. Yet his presence was never mentioned by Greene or Ritter, although surely the Monster's connection—yes, relationship—with the Frankenstein family had to be known to them. I knew well from my hours over the letters the sinister force and the cunning mind that must be behind the Greenes of this world. While my aspirations for recovering the information my father had gained at such sacrifice were unaltered, the prospects of success under these onerous circumstances were as unlikely as the camel's passing through the needle's eye. And now the venture was moving in a dangerous direction. "Revolution?" I asked. The word roved through my brain like the heaviest particle, spinning off with the centrifugal force of worry.

"Greene sounds very militant, as though he is a military man, and William responds in a similar way. They talk of supplies and men, and they are somehow using the mountain peasants to support their ambitions."

"On behalf of the Monster?"

"The Monster is behind the whole thing. But there is a problem, and you have a vital role to play. Oh, Victor, the whole matter is evil. Promise that you will free yourself of this at the earliest moment."

"I do promise. Somehow we will persevere, darling, and when this nightmare ends, as it must, we will wed and settle far from the reach of any recurrence of this cursed evil."

"Victor, such happy thoughts will sustain me. I want so much to be your wife."

There was a loud cough from William. "The horses are coming up the path."

I picked up the saddlebags and went out onto the porch. Felicia followed with the medical bag, which I attached to the saddle horn. There was a small blanket roll behind the saddle.

"Are your medical supplies in order?" asked Greene.

"The case is in its usual condition. Whether it is sufficient depends on the demands."

Greene scowled again. "You still have almost four hours of daylight," he said. "Time enough for you to reach the mountain trail and for William to return in the dusk. You will reach your destination in just two days."

"How will I know?"

"The trail? Digby will set you right. Once on the

high meadow called the Downs, you will find stone piles marking the trail."

"I am not concerned about that. I need to know how I will know when I have arrived. Who will meet me?"

"Just follow the instructions. You will know quickly enough when you are to go no further. Move along steadily and faithfully. Otherwise . . ."

"I weary of your threats, Greene," I said, swinging up on the saddle.

Greene scowled in his most dangerous manner, hands on hips, revealing both a pistol and a sheathed knife. William was on the other horse, and a pistol was prominent on his belt. The German shepherd was at the rear. At a sign from Greene, he barked and the horses moved off at a trot. I barely had time to turn in the saddle and wave farewell to Felicia before we were out of sight of the cottage and moving down a mottled path of shade and sunshine, headed toward the base of the nearby mountains. We skirted a river bed full of cabin-sized boulders. The stream was dry, save the middle, where the 20-foot-wide water flowed placidly, having fallen a hundred feet from a spectacular waterfall. I would have stopped under any other circumstances to admire the view.

William led the way at a brisk pace, the path being broad and easy to follow. He avoided conversation for the first half hour, until we came to a turnpike, where he slowed and fell back beside me.

"William," I said, "tell me about your decision to leave your employ without due notice to my poor aunt, who has need of your services in her old age, to fall in with these colonials for what ends."

"It was not as difficult, Doctor, as you may imagine. I could see the sands of my life run out with no hope of advancement of my lot in that feudal society."

"Come, William. You were well treated."

"That is a blind spot of the upper classes," he responded. "In your eyes my treatment was good. But it was at your pleasure, as though I were a dog. There was no recognition of my rights as a man. Nor was there any hope of social justice in England. In America, perhaps, if the old prejudices are avoided as the country progresses. There is room here for more diversity. It was easy for me to make the choice when it was offered."

"Offered?"

"By Greene, of course. He noticed my qualities immediately. I have come to respect his goals and ability."

"And what are those?" I asked.

"Goals? They are not mine to disclose. Ability? Greene is a superb organizer and planner. He works hard and treats those around him fairly."

"He beat me."

"Precisely to my point," responded William and spurred on his chestnut mount to a faster speed.

Each hour we rested the horses for a few minutes. As dusk was falling, William turned off the turnpike as though he had been there before and I followed. There in a grove was a rushing stream. We dismounted and tethered the horses. The German shepherd kept its bright eyes on me. "You will spend the night here and, in the morning, continue on. You will be under observation and there is no need for me to accompany you further. I have urgent work to do."

"You seem to enjoy your assignment, whatever it is."

"I have responsibility and prospects that I have never had before. I mean to serve them well and earn a place of power and importance."

"It is already dark," I complained. "I'll be fortunate to find wood for a fire."

"Your privileged youth, Doctor, your summers in Scotland, should stand you well. I need not repeat, I suspect, the injunction to do as you have been ordered." He sat straight in the saddle, and in my mind's eye I could see his scarlet coat and saber of an army that had discarded him. "The path up the mountain is dangerous. At the top is the Downs, a meadow with bogs and trails, at an altitude of about 5,000 feet. You will learn the details as you experience them."

And with that he was off, the dog running along behind. I was alone. I did not want to be. There was nothing to do but confront my jumbled thoughts, and this I needed to avoid.

I removed the saddlebags from the horse, as well as the medical bag and the blanket roll. Dry wood was easier to find than I had thought, but I was concerned that the rising wind would make the fire difficult to control. I groped for stones and finally set up a crude circle of them, piled wood and leaves, which were dust dry, in the center, and lit the blaze with two matches. My spirits rose with the smoke. I leaned on a tree and ate jerkin beef and an apple, while I debated again whether to arm myself with my pistol or leave it concealed. Somehow the weight of the weapon in my pocket would be reassuring, so that I would not feel so completely in the power of the Fiend—although just what I would do with the gun that would make these problems vanish I knew not. A magic wand would be in better order, for only that would right this wrong situation. I decided to leave the gun where it was against a future occasion. So far in my experience with the Fiend, I had been outwitted at every turn. Surprised, beaten, kept off balance so that the initiative and the changing of the scene were in the hands of my enemies. How could I alter this grim tableau so that the actors would be directed by me and not by others?

I was reluctant to allow the fire to die, providing as it did a link with civilization and humanity. But tiny sparks were being continually carried off into the night and I feared a fire. Accordingly, I walked to the stream, filled my canteen with water, and extinguished the fire. My blanket roll was on a fairly flat spot, and the promise of a long night's sleep was inviting. Or so it seemed. With every snapped twig or animal call I sat up and strained my eyes into the darkness. There was no doubt whatsoever. If he wanted my life, he would have it. I could no more resist his will this night than a leaf in a stream can contend with the current.

CHAPTER V

THE DOWNS

MY SLEEP was the sleep of despair. I awoke with a chill, to find that dew had settled on my blankets. There was a faint lightness in the grove, penetrating a heavy fog. My mount was standing by the tree where I had tethered him, asleep. I rolled up the soggy blankets, cinched on the saddle, and reloaded the gear. The fog was thick in the trees, like strips of cotton Christmas decorations. The horse settled on a fast walking pace up the trail, which was wide enough for a wagon but suffered from disuse. The rains and snows, freezes and thaws, had eroded it badly.

By nine o'clock on my gold watch—an heirloom from Captain Walton's father—the fog was, if anything, heavier. I had expected it to lift as we rose up from the valley. The deterioration of the trail was becoming more pronounced as the elevation and angle increased. I slowed the pace for fear of sliding off the trail onto the jagged rocks and into the stream I could hear running to my left. For another hour we—the horse and I—climbed in this cautious manner, until we came to the first ridge line of perhaps 1,500 feet. Suddenly the sun burst clear of the higher clouds and fell on the fog like a maid sweeping the kitchen. Within minutes I could catalogue the vista. Back to my left, cliffs on the other side of the valley floor rose about 4,000 feet, the top 500 feet of sheer perpendicular stone, like a great wall with towers and battlements. The sun, striking obliquely, cast deep shadows across these walls, heightening the illusion of a fortress. As the trail turned, the vista toward the Downs opened. There again was the same phenomenon, the battlements and buttresses of solid rock, as though guarding the entrance to a kingdom.

Water poured from the rock walls along the trail, and I dismounted to give the horse an opportunity to drink. It had been cold when we left, but already, with the sun in full force, I had given thought to removing my coat. Now, in the shadow, it was chilly again, and the hot breath of the horse rose off the pool wherein he slacked his thirst. I gave him an apple and ate one myself, more of a delay than a demand for food. As we rose ever higher, we came out again into the sun, now much closer to the plateau Greene had called the Downs. The very top of the Downs, above the rock battlements, was studded with spruce and pine, reinforcing the impression of an impenetrable redoubt. The rock cliffs looked cruel, marching in their serried ranks, shades of gray and shadows cut through over the ages by the stream that was lost to view below in a deep gorge. The Downs apparently were the highest point around, although mountains of similar height extended back and back to the horizon. The mountains and the forests stretched endlessly toward the western frontier of America. The Downs themselves seemed bypassed by time and circumstance.

An hour later there was a wooden sign, with a warning burned into it to endure against the extremes of the weather: "Bridge Out." I went on nonetheless, admiring the opposite cliffs. I remembered my father's description to Captain Walton of the Fiend's crawling straight up the overhanging side of Mont Salève in the Alps. I found my eye fastening on what seemed to be movement on the far rock face, but before I could tell whether something was moving—a bird, a falling rock, a shadow—we had moved beyond where I could keep the spot under observation. Both the horse and I were becoming more apprehensive each step up the road. The sun found one of the few clouds in the otherwise bright July day, and as the shadows deepened on rock and trail and the leaves rustled in a sudden gust of wind swirling wildly from the top of the shadowy canyon walls, my spirits fell in the gloom.

The ruined ends of the bridge now came to view. The leading abutments were charred by fire. I tethered the horse to a tree and went forward to reconnoiter. Below the bridge, at least 100 feet, ran a stream. Building such a bridge to begin with was a feat of primitive engineering; therefore, I could comprehend the reluctance of whoever owned the high meadows of the Downs to undertake the repair and reconstruction. Yet neatly laid across the bridge, and neatly spanning the distance, were four giant logs, squared by an adze on one side. How much did such logs weigh? Who could have put them there? I shuddered, knowing the only possible answer.

I would have preferred that the span were wider. I adjusted the blinders on the horse as narrowly as possible and, stepping carefully, led him behind me out onto the bridge. A powerful feeling of vertigo and nausea began to overcome me once I glanced below, despite my intentions, instinct in the end being the master. The dancing waters surged through rocks in powerful rapids. I stumbled as the horse neighed loudly, almost frightening both of us off the bridge.

At the last moment I did slip, but managed to yank the bridle and the horse to safety, though I fell to the ground myself, breathing heavily. Rising on my arm, I peered down, down into the chasm and the boiling stream. My sense of panic was increasing. I expected a sign, a whisper, a threat, if not confrontation. The only things on the trail were fresh-cut grass and a woven grass basket of apples. The horse saw them first, and it was with difficulty that I retrieved the apples. I did not want a sick horse to contend with. The beast chomped the grass with passing manners, taking, however, about fifteen minutes before being well satisfied. The trail was especially slippery, water seeping everywhere from rocks along the bank, so I led my mount for another spell before putting foot to stirrup.

The sun was now bright and hot again, and I tied my coat across the saddle horn. My morale improved despite myself as I looked again across the valley leading to the walls of the Downs.

Constantly in my thoughts on this curious mission was the brief conversation the previous day with Felicia. How much I loved her, how dear her concerns! She was real. The Monster was unreal. Perhaps he really did not exist. After all, can anyone but God create life? There was the rub. What if the story of my father's work was really hallucination—what if the Monster had never really come to life, had never opened his "dull yellow eye," but all of it was an impression created by a condition of overwork? These questions were hopes—escapes from the reality, however bizarre, that I faced with averted eyes.

Finally, I had to prepare myself in all seriousness and fear and humility to meet the Monster. Greene's device of leaving me in the wilds alone was intended simply to increase my final vulnerability. The Monster must have learned much over the past thirty years. And once again, what did he really want of me? What he had wanted from my father—a female monster to share his fate, to multiply in these isolated reaches and strike down at a moment of his choosing on the objects of his hate and envy? Fortunately, I had not the slightest idea how to construct a mate for the Monster. Could he, however, force me to do so against my will? Or would the Monster's demands be more subtle? The motive on my part that was driving me onward toward this meeting with the Monster was absolutely clear in my mind. Whether I could succeed at my self-appointed task was another matter, but I was determined to try.

Or was I? The bright sun placed me in an altogether different mood than had the fog in the early morning. There were still choices. I did not need to speed to my doom like a lemming headed toward the sea. True, my curiosity was my guide, but a rational mind, dried by the sunlight, has a powerful interest in survival. And that was the feeling that suddenly seized me. The turnpike was a logical escape route. Surely there was substantial traffic on the road. I could find help, arouse the authorities and return to the Berkeley Springs Inn to rescue Felicia and undo the plot of Greene and my unfaithful servant. In a twinkling, I blamed my weakness on the sea voyage and on my confused mental state for not having moved decisively on this matter. I cursed myself for a fool, reined in the horse, and resolutely retraced the trail toward the highway.

My spirits rose with each step of the retreat. I had regained control of my mental processes, no longer mesmerized. The stakes were simply too high in this matter to risk trying to combat or cope with the Monster on his own grounds and under his own terms. There was no way to accomplish that. Let him rot or thrive, die or procreate, in his abominable hills, while the rest of civilized society went its own way. Let the secrets of his wretched creation die with him. For I was increasingly convinced that without such an outcome his victims would fill the pages of our history books. It was with difficulty that I restrained the horse to a fast walk, in deference to the slippery trail.

Rounding another bend, we at last approached the bridge, and I dismounted. To my chagrin and horror, the four logs had disappeared. There was no way to span the gorge from the trail. The descent from the path to try at a lower level was so perilous that one brief glance was enough to determine the impossibility of my escape plan. Fresh cuts in the bank showed that the logs had been levered into the stream and carried off in the tumultuous river. That instrument must have been close at hand, watching. Dazed, I once again found myself astride the horse, retracing the trail up the mountain, weighted down by a leaden heart.

It was nearly two o'clock when I reached the Downs, where the trail ran out in the scrub and bushes and bog that were immediately ahead. Right at the end of the trail was another pile of cut grass. After a short rest while the horse was eating, I mounted him again and started out into the trackless Downs. The small stone piles to mark the trail were simple and clever. The stones could easily be scattered and there would be no track and no trace of where the trail had gone. For I could see after a hundred yards that without those small piles of three or four stones rising above the brambly ground cover, I would never be able to find my way again along this identical trail.

The bogs were full of low berry bushes and lichens and mosses of all descriptions. The trail passed through the bogs into firmer ground, covered by small pines and spruce trees, the second growth of an earlier logging. But on across the rise and into the next valley, there were magnificent tree specimens, like the masts of sailing ships. There were signs of beaver: small pools dammed and trees of all dimensions cut off by the unmistakable gnawing of the sharp-toothed animals. Aside from the cawing of crows, there were no cries of birds. All the berry bushes suggested bear, but none was in evidence.

After an hour's ride through this idyllic countryside, the sun hung in the west as though pierced by a mountaintop. As the penetration increased, it slowly became dusk, a dappling of purple and pink clouds off to the west as the sun's rays, no longer directly visible, turned heavenward like a powerful but fading lamp. The sounds of rushing water, a low controlled roar like the approach of a distant steam engine, became louder. I started down into the next valley, where I could see a few hundred yards away a small stream, still mainly concealed by a heavy growth of bushy pines. Once upon it, I perceived that the water level was low and that the water had a reddish hue from minerals in the rocks. Aside from the pools and eddies where I paused, the stream still had considerable force and vigor as it plunged on down toward the principal river in the plateau.

The rocks in the stream stood out like flagstones. I dismounted and followed them to the other side, leading my horse, slipping only once and wetting my boots. On the most promising level spot for a campsite, there was a pile of wood. I took this to indicate that I should stop there, the Fiend having accurately plotted the amount of time it would take me to reach this distance. (Had he known I would try to turn back?) There was no shortage of combustible materials in the area. Along the bank of the stream were flat rocks devoid of vegetation, which made it safe to light a fire without the risk of touching off the tinderlike ground cover of leaves and pine cones. To ensure that I could control the fire, I again moved stones into a crude circle, then picked up pine cones and leaves and twigs and set a match to them, gradually adding larger pieces. Soon I had a splendid fire, which warmed my spirits and aching bones. I was not used to so much riding and walking in a single day, which, along with the psychic distress I was suffering, combined to reduce me to a state of acute fatigue.

It was not until I sat down and pulled the jerkin beef from the blanket roll that I began to realize exactly how tired I was—how completely exhausted physically, emotionally, and mentally. The Fiend no doubt had planned it that way—for whatever purpose he had, he would come upon me in a helpless plight and work his will. Yet he could have waylaid me long ago if he wished. No, he had something else in mind, something more sinister, more dangerous than anything he had tried previously.

I spread the still damp blankets on the ground over a scooped-up pile of leaves and stretched my throbbing limbs. It was just eight o'clock, but it was dark as the bowels of death, save for the stars. They were absolutely brilliant—Venus, the Milky Way, the Big Dipper, Orion and his warlike pose. I looked all about me, awash in the light at the edge of darkness. The river reflected the brightest members, leaving me alone with my thoughts which cascaded like a stream into the night. The fire burned down, and the intensity of the darkness increased. There was no wind, so I did not extinguish the fire. It was a comfort, a product of my own creation. There was no use in smothering it to hide from the Fiend. If he were watching or wanted to find me, he could do that with or without the fire. I lay on my back between the lumpy blankets, losing myself in the heavens.

Again I rose at dawn and pursued the way as in a trance. The trail went steadily upward from the river toward a clump of dense pines. Short of the trees, on the bank, was a huge wooden cross. I thought immediately of the Druids and Stonehenge. But I knew instinctively of the hand that must have set it in place. It spoke of a monster even more complex than my father had ever dealt with—the ruler of my current destiny. The cross protruded thirty feet above the rocks, and the cross arm, notched into the upright, extended twenty feet. There was bird dung, both old and fresh, on the crossbar. I had not thought the wretch would have displayed such an ostentatious monument to his presence. It was an indication that he was fully confident in himself. The cross was no warning, but more like a claim. Those who would contest it would face his right of eminent domain.

I stayed in front of the cross for some time, trying to determine its significance, being unsatisfied with my initial reaction. What really did it mean? Why had he erected it? My mind was too drawn out, too fragmented, to try to piece together such complex external observations. So I moved on, advancing toward the far northern end of the valley. I periodically heard sharp noises. It took me a moment to fix these new sounds and relate them to my experience. There had been little the first day but the cawing of crows. But no, there was no mistake—it was the sound of dogs barking. I stopped and moved my head slowly, trying to determine the precise direction. Dogs. Wolves? I had no idea whether wolves lived in this part of America, or, for that matter, what the sound of a wolf would be like. Yes, the barks sounded like domesticated dogs, faint in the wind, blowing from the south and west. Was I to find a settlement, the Monster in a domestic scene?

But his collecting dogs would make sense. Dogs would be as friendly to the Monster as to any other. Food, affection, and they would be loyal to him. Dogs would not regard the Fiend with human eyes or concern themselves with moral questions, the brutal crimes and his tortured self-justification. They would provide companionship and play a role in finding food, although his tastes had once run to nuts and berries, anything coarse. I wondered for a moment what kind of stomach he had, from what man or beast. The Downs were full of game, as deer tracks had shown in the boggy parts. But the barking of dogs, now clearly louder, was unsettling, and the urge to escape before the dread confrontation was overpowering. Escape, however, was not for me. My throat was dry and, despite the heat of the day, my teeth chattered uncontrollably.

The sounds became louder, and I was certain that his settlement was beyond the next ridge. I dismounted, again tethering the horse, and walked cautiously along the edge of the stream, jumping from rock to rock. Several hundred yards ahead the sound of water increased, and I conjectured that the stream would merge with another, probably the one where I had spent the night. I was on the east side of the stream, still in the sun, when I heard, "Welcome, son of Victor Frankenstein." The whisper! The voice sounded as though it were in my ear, and I spun around, nearly losing my balance. I clutched wildly in the air, trying to hold a trace of the source. It had come from the opposite bank, from the shade and shadow. I raised my hand to my eyes, the better to peer into the shadows. There in a massive black fur, sitting on a log, was the Monster himself, a hulk of a form, shapeless like rubble, a bearskin covering his upper torso, the head of the bear hanging down incongruously over his shoulder. Though I could not readily make out the Fiend's features, they were etched in acid in my brain.

He motioned to me to cross the stream. "Be not afraid, Frankenstein. I welcome you to my kingdom." His arm slowly, feebly, fell to his side. "I have much to talk to you about, and I seek your understanding and assistance."

Shivering as though I had the ague, I picked my way

across the twenty yards of rapids, jumping into the cold of the shade. The Monster was another thirty steps or so downstream and a similar distance up the bank. He held up his great arm for me to halt. "Look at me, Frankenstein. Do not shield your eyes. Clad in this manner, seated in shadow, my deformities are hidden and my body warmed. It is strange, is it not, that the appearance of a wild beast is more pleasant to your eye than the face created by your own father? I had wondered how you would look. Not misshapen as I, rejected by the human race, but with fine features, resembling those of your father. But not I. His pattern for me was horrendous."

"Beauty is in the eye of the beholder," I replied, "and you should be grateful for life itself. The fact that you, of whatever clay, are participating in the higher form of life should merit your gratitude."

"Your lack of understanding of my problem is greater than your father's."

"No more than he will I participate in your foul schemes."

"Foul schemes?" The Daemon paused and held his head in his huge hands. "Do you mean, perchance, my desire for a mate?" He laughed a hollow laugh, not greatly different from Greene's, as though the two had taken lessons in another cave from a witch. "So it was. I have, however, traveled for many years since those now dreary, unhappy days. I have seen the mating of the universe, the coupling of beasts of all species, and then, one dewy dawn, the coupling of two of different species. And I have read. And the satyr is not the least of God's more complicated animals. No, Frankenstein. I have grown older and wiser. If one must satiate his sexual thirst, there is no lack of containers." He once again laughed his hollow laugh, and the chill down my spine was as cold as ice itself.

"Come, Frankenstein," the Monster taunted. "What do you have to say about the facts of procreation in this brutal world? And what do you say about compassion for the misdeed of your father?"

Before I answered, half a dozen armed men, rifles slung casually over their shoulders, appeared beside him, coming out of the shadows or from a cave barred from my vision by sun and shade. One advanced on me. In the sunlight I recognized the Reverend Ritter, his face strained and pinched. "He insisted on waiting for you, having had this day on his mind for months. He is in desperate circumstances and needs your assistance immediately."

"What am I to do?"

"He is gravely wounded. A hunter mistook him for a wild animal and shot him. This was months ago, and despite his extraordinary strength he has not recovered. His blood has been ebbing away, and there has been no satisfactory method to replace it. What you sent was not sufficient."

The situation clarified in my mind instantly. He had been nearly dead from loss of blood or fluid, and then the arsenic poisoning.

Ritter held my arm. "He is willing to forgive the past, and you should be also."

"But of the future?"

"If you succeed, Frankenstein," said the metallic voice, "I shall be indebted to you for a comparable boon."

I looked into Ritter's eyes, which had lost their redness. His voice was calm and persuasive, almost cultured.

No longer did he speak the slurred common tongue of our previous meeting. The Monster was being carried back into a cave, and my medical bag, which I had left on the saddle of my horse, was being carried in the same direction. "You must do this," said Ritter, "for many things depend upon it. The dream of my entire congregation, all these simple mountain folk, requires from you speedy and successful help for our afflicted savior." He touched my shoulder and raised his hand to the sky. " 'Blessed are they that do his commandments, that they may have right to the tree of life, and may enter in through the gates into the city.' " He cast his eyes about, then toward the men struggling to help the Monster into the cave. " 'The grace of our Lord Jesus Christ be with you all. Amen.' "

I followed Ritter toward the cave in a stupor of fear and curiosity, the last words of the Book of Revelation ringing in my ears.

CHAPTER VI

THE CULT

THE FIRST TWENTY-FOUR HOURS in the Monster's lair sorely tried my stamina and my faith in eventual extrication from this unholy scene. Led by Ritter and mentally prodded by the armed men, I entered the crude cave. It was fairly light and well ventilated by air pouring in from shallow shafts that reached its interior. There was a view from the entrance down the stream, although no other signs of habitation were visible. The human activity was beyond the ridge.

The Monster had been placed on a large wooden table which would serve as an operating table. Another table hard by held lamps and medical instruments, chemicals, and my own bag open for my inspection and use. The Monster beckoned and I drew near, beyond the range of his enfeebled grasp, for I was unsure what those watery yellow eyes meant in my regard. His voice was calm, although its unnaturalness chilled my being and I was pressed to concentrate on his instructions.

"My decision to bring you here, Frankenstein, was

not lightly taken. You have solved the riddle of the fluid that occupies my veins, not the blood of humans, so that there is quite literally no medical practitioner who can do me service. And beyond that there is the need to guard the knowledge of my presence from those who may be hostile to me. My treatment at the hands of mankind is a long and cruel story."

"On your bed of pain I will not contradict you, though on behalf of my family I reserve agreement."

"You must succeed, Frankenstein—if not for my sake, then for your own. My warrant is all that will send you safely home." He closed his eyes and rested his great body, fully eight feet long. The bearskin removed, he was clad in a simple robe of cotton cloth, fashioned from sheets.

Two women entered now with Ritter to function as nurses. They too were dressed in white sheets. The one was a typical inbred rustic; the other, however, was a dark-skinned beauty, large black eyes and long black hair tied severely in the back in a bun fastened with two mother-of-pearl hairpins. Hot water and cloths were at hand. My first task was to assay the wound. With the aid of the dark-haired woman, whose hands showed training and ability, I inspected the wound below the right knee where a rifle bullet had entered. There was a purple oozing about the wound, not a rot of gangrene, which would long ago have been fatal, but an ugly, pulsating, oozing glob.

"He has not allowed anyone to attend to this, fearing it might worsen."

"The slow seepage has saved him," I replied.

"The new fluid helped, although he did not respond as I had hoped."

"How did you use it?"

"I injected it in small quantities daily by syringe," she replied.

So that was the answer. In small doses, his body would accommodate the quantity of arsenic, undetected by this unsuspecting nursing aide.

"I will set about to undo the damage," I said. Once the fluid formula was mixed and placed over a charcoal fire to boil, I set about to make the repair. There was to be no chloroform, Ritter advised, and I could tell by the Monster's reaction to the probe that none was needed. The lead bullet removed, I now turned my attention to stopping the flow of fluid that had continued for months. The wound had been acute, the ball having smashed into the leg, pulverizing arteries, veins, and muscle. My tentative conclusion on noting the feeble pulse of the Monster and his present condition was that the vital fluid simply could not be regenerated by the body itself. His "blood" supply was circulating through a closed system of tubing, large and strong veins and arteries, so that if a leak developed, there was danger that the whole system would simply drain away. But if that were so, how would the rest of the body function as it did? The answer to this must lie in my father's notes, and unless I found them, the secret of this Monster would never be known. The task of suturing the veins and arteries was tedious, with the relatively dim light and the willing but not quite professional help. But at last it was done, and the leg was properly bandaged.

I then set about to reheat the cooled fluid, with Jenny's help. She was the dark one and had, she said, taken nursing training in Baltimore for two years. She had explained this in a tone of apology for her relative inexperience, but I considered her work excellent and praised her, which pleased her immensely. It remained for the solution to cool for the second time. I would allow Jenny to handle the injections, which had to be massive to restore the fluid to its proper level and thus restore the strength of my enemy, the murderer of my father's family. I was grateful for her presence, because the effort of the day had drained my resources, and my strength ebbed as that of the Monster rose.

It was Ritter who led me out of the cave for a respite. The stars were again hung like lanterns in the sky, and the night noises of cicadas and frogs blended through the valley. There were the yips of dogs and the sound of voices a hundred yards or so further on. I sat down heavily on an overturned tree, torn out by its roots from a previous storm or possibly a flood current.

"Dr. Frankenstein, I congratulate you on your work. Our friend will fully recover, I am certain, and his work will flourish, if God so wills."

"The nurses were essential," I responded. "They performed nobly, especially the darker one, Jenny."

"She has handled the medical problems here almost on her own. The people love her, which sits poorly with Greene."

"Why so?"

"She is his wife, you see, and Greene wants no one to have a claim, a hold, that could in some way interfere with his position."

"But his wife?"

"There are rumors of dissension. But that concerns

me not. I am deeply grateful for your help in saving the life of our friend, who has meant so much to me."

"And his work?"

Ritter was silent. His manner was strange. Then he moved closer. "First I must make a confession. I have a great weakness which the Lord so far has not seen fit to cure. I am at this moment useless. Can you help me?"

"What is it that you want of me?"

"Alcohol. Do you have in your medical case grain alcohol that will lay to rest, even for an hour, the turmoil in my soul?" I went to my medical bag and produced a small bottle from my supplies, the solvent for most of my prescriptions. Ritter drank it down in a mighty gulp, and I feared for his liver and for his life. But he seemed unfazed by the experience, and became more animated. "It was in the spring, at Easter time, that my path crossed with that of this giant man in extraordinary circumstances. I have been preaching in these parts for the past five years, my church being further to the west, on down in the valley beyond these Downs. I had frankly hoped for something different when I graduated from the seminary in Baltimore, but even then it was God's will that liquor would control my life, and that habit led me to this poverty-cursed region of simple but God-fearing folk."

The alcohol was now going into his blood stream, and his excitement grew as he recalled the circumstances. "As so often happens in these parts, the wetness of spring brings on the fevers and agues, and this year was no exception. Except it was like a pestilence, and of the sixty souls in my congregation, fully forty died within the early part of April—including my wife, who had long borne my burden for me. The survivors were hard pressed to dig the graves and shape the coffins, so horrible was the pestilence and so rapid and sure its deadly results. On the eve of Easter Sunday I went to church and prayed all night, going to the graveyard at dawn to be near my wife. And there, rising among the tombstones like a tree, was this giant of a man."

"You were not afraid?"

"My courage at that moment came from the bottle I had been drinking through the night. I asked him his name, which he said he couldn't give me since he didn't have one, and his purpose, which he said was to bring hope where there was none and to help those who needed it the most."

The conversation had lasted for an hour, Ritter said, and several points had been brought to light. The Monster told him of his own creation, that he was a being made through man's genius and that he had the secret of life in his possession. "Can you imagine my joy in hearing this message as the sun rose on Easter Day—when in the depths of gloom, with no tears left to offer my flock, I met a being wet with dew and full of compassion who offered to set things right?"

"An amazing offer indeed!"

"If your tone is one of skepticism, Dr. Frankenstein, then it is misplaced. I have utter faith in our friend, and he will, as in the Psalms, restore our souls."

"You mean that he has requickened your dead?"

"Not yet. But in the face of the living evidence that he has the secret of life, there is no reason to doubt. We have removed the dead from our valley and brought them here for the process. It would have long been completed, except for his injury which you have now made right."

I shuddered at this prospect, if I understood it properly. Obtaining corpses had always been difficult in England and America as well, for scientific purposes of course, and had led to the practice of grave robbing to obtain cadavers. The brazenness of the Monster in bargaining with a minister for the whole churchyard of dead was on the same scale with his previously known treacheries.

"Are you saying that this Monster has promised you that he will restore these dead to the quick, bring them back to life?"

"That is his promise, and that is our belief. He is after all a miracle in his own right. He was born without sin. He has the God-given knowledge of how to accomplish this miracle and he will do so on our behalf."

Born without sin. Not the original sin, that is true. But I already knew that he was born from refuse, the offal of the charnel house, this soulless creature of no sense of right or wrong, a cleverness that passed for kindness to these simple folk, and cunning that knew no moral ends. I shuddered.

"Our entire congregation has moved to the Downs until the miracle is accomplished. Then we will return to our homes and spread the word of this miracle."

"Where is this work taking place?" I asked.

Ritter was feeling the full effects of the alcohol, and he answered with the slur of our first encounter. "I am not to say, but it is in another cave, larger than the one here, large enough to accommodate all those dead. I tell you, Frankenstein, if you had experienced this spring, with those who were closest and dearest, you would, as I do, support this work with all your energy and prayer."

The idea was so grotesque that without the fact of the Monster's presence just inside the cave, I would have considered it a simple hallucination or, in Ritter's case, the inevitable effect of alcohol.

"You are not attempting to dissuade me, are you, from believing our friend's story?" asked Ritter. "You are further evidence, almost as miraculous, having come to this remote scene to save your father's creation."

"It is not that, Reverend Ritter. I am not denying the tale. But I cannot vouchsafe that the Monster will be able to do what he says, regardless of his intentions."

Ritter grabbed my collar and shook me. "I have given too much, Frankenstein—too much for anything to go wrong." With that he lurched into the darkness toward the sound of human voices, leaving me alone.

I returned immediatel to the cave. Jenny had transferred the first gallon. The Monster's pulse continued weak and he was almost comatose, but I knew from my readings that he could survive in such a condition, weak as he seemed to be, and that by dawn, when the next batch of fluid was ready, I would be able to make the final transfer. After that, his recuperation should be complete within days.

I motioned to Jenny to follow me back outside. She was drawn from her work, but the lines on her features were light and her resiliency was certain. I admired the fineness of her bones and the strength of her slightness.

"All went well," I said rhetorically, in lieu of other questions and concerns that were welling up in my brain.

"Yes, very well. Better, I think, than before. He now seems more composed, breathing easier than previously."

"Good," I lied. "This work must be a burden on you, considering all the other labor piled upon your shoulders."

"The people here? Yes, I could use more assistance, of course, but I do not mind the burden. Other things bear me down, not the relief of suffering." She then began to tremble. The cool of the mountain was upon us, and I instinctively drew her near me. She nestled against me like a small animal, a kitten, and was warm on my breast. Then she drew back, still holding me by the arms. "Please help. Me above all. Please help." Her eyes pleaded with me, for a cause I knew not.

"How?"

"I can't say . . . not yet. Not now. Let me think."

She turned back into the cave. I followed shortly, but I did not see her in the dimly lighted room, where the pine torches provided the only illumination.

The sleeping arrangements were primitive. I was simply given a blanket and a hard bench. The guards remained in the room; some were asleep, but no doubt there was more systematic watching than was evident. There was a certain laxness about the place, however, that gave me hope of escaping if my freedom and that of Felicia were not readily granted. I brooded over the picture Ritter had painted. The culmination of this ominous experiment awaited only the recovery of the Monster, which would not be long in coming, unless . . . There were poisons in my bag beyond alcohol and arsenic. Indeed, there was a small flask of cyanide solution which I had prepared when I considered a problem of extermination in Aunt Margaret's basement. It was still there, I was certain. Would an injection of such a solution into the vitals of the Monster end his wretched life? And if so, would I immediately be apprehended and in that way trade my life for his? Did I want to do that? The fact that I was now considering the prospect showed the extent to which Ritter's story had penetrated my consciousness, my awareness again that the Monster had to be eliminated at whatever cost. Perhaps it was possible that he could do what he had told Ritter and bring these people back to life. But in what condition, and what form? Ritter was expecting one thing, but I was suspecting another. Then there was also Jenny. Was there a simpler and happier solution in that direction?

Another dawn. The crowing of roosters heralded the civilization that lay just beyond my sight. My eyes opened on my nemesis.

"Good morning, Doctor. I understand you have performed capably so far." Greene was still dressed in his odd costume, with the round broad-brimmed hat. Jenny had evidently reported on the operation and transfusion.

While I was not elated to see him, there was the possibility that the rest of the party, including Felicia, had come to the Downs, probably by a different route.

"I should be through before the morning is past," I said, rising and moving to the crude table of medical supplies. I found the syringe and injection needle and noticed that the cyanide bottle, clearly labeled, was missing. My eye went from the empty space in the case to Greene, which was a mistake. He met my glance and read my thoughts as clearly as if I had written them on a sheet of paper. There was nothing now to do but inject the fluid, which I did slowly. Over the course of two hours, I transferred almost two gallons of it into the hulk of the Fiend. His breathing and pulse gradually improved, and by the time I was finished, he had opened his dull eyes and contorted his thin purplish lips into what was supposed to be a smile. His carved even ivorylike teeth showed, and he spoke again in that spine-chilling accent. "My strength is returning, Frankenstein. Your delay has cost me precious time, but I am nonetheless grateful for your service, no matter that it was given with reluctance and misgiving."

Greene stepped forward and said, "I have been assured that your injection was given with complete safety, last night through the office of my wife and today under my vigilance. But I would not recommend further medications from the son of your old antagonist."

"His service and movement are to be restricted. And aside from one remaining matter, I think our need for him will effectively be over."

I packed my medical bag and was led from the cave by Greene. Outside stood William, a sword at his belt and a pistol on his hip. He was flanked by two men dressed in black. William was treated with deference, and I could only assume that he was in a position of command over this motley band of local mercenaries.

"Digby will show you to your quarters, Franken-stein," said Greene. "He is responsible for your safe-keeping while you are with us. So I would judge it wise that you heed his advice."

I shrugged my understanding of Greene's instruction and fell in behind William Digby, a gimpy soldier, while the two men in black followed. As we crossed the ridge, we entered the settlement—a collection of log houses of rustic charm, about three dozen altogether, set in a square, with women working in front of some of them on domestic chores. From further out in the valley came the sound of flintlocks firing.

"Training, William?"

He ground his teeth over my refusal to play the Digby game. "Hunting," was his quick reply.

He marched me to a solid storehouse. There was already a guard posted at the door, and along with him the German shepherd, still salivating and tongue moving back and forth like a reptile. We had the capacity to unnerve each other. He rose and moved off as I entered the storehouse. The bolt was slammed home from the outside, and I was again a prisoner. The windows were barred to secure the stacks of provisions, and all were shuttered, save two.

In the dim light I recognized the gunpowder from our wagon trip as well as the kegs of salt, flour, and sugar. Other boxes stacked in the single large room were unmarked. Near them was a cot, and I immediately went to it, placing my medical bag beside it, pulling off my boots, and flinging myself down to rest. Amidst the cheery voices of the women and the distant sound of shooting, I napped. Only the heat of noon woke me up, perspiring. And then the door opened and Felicia entered, smiling, with a hamper of food. "One hour—one hour and no more," said the guard.

We clung together in the middle of the room, savoring the feeling of our bodies one to the other. I absorbed the fragrance of her shining hair. She was enthusiastic. "I know we will be leaving here once the Monster definitely recovers."

"And how do you know that?" I asked.

"Greene has taken me to him. Had I not known what to expect, I would have expired. But he is better. He is grateful to you for your assistance and has asked me to help nurse him back to health. And after that, we are free to go."

"He said that?"

"He said he would no longer need us."

My face showed my suspicion.

"Do you mean you are trying to fathom something other than what he said?" she asked, smiling. "That is what he meant, just what he said. We will be leaving soon."

Though the room was large, I was nonetheless reluctant to speak frankly in a situation where the walls might have ears. I took her hand and led her to the cot, where I sat her down and looked deeply into her eyes. "Darling, I beg you to recall the essence of my poor father's experience with the Fiend, the product of his creativity. How can you doubt that in the end he would have preferred to have achieved nothing at all?"

"Ah, Victor, the happenstance of our previous experience gives me confidence to say that all is well with this creature. He has absorbed, I believe, the reason that he is here and, because of his capabilities, his obligation to humanity to stay where he is. And once his health is restored, he has no purchase on you or me. We will be free to leave, to start a new life."

I wept. I could not restrain the bitter tears, the aching in my brain, that cried out to stay the evils of the Monster.

But how would I explain my knowledge and fears to others—recruit those of opposite persuasion? "My dear, the goals of this menage are unclear to me, except that there can only be one consummation—the triumph of their evil over the goodness of our charity and love."

I quickly told her of my brief encounter with Ritter and Greene's wife. Felicia's brow furrowed, but her interest, her fascination, returned to the Monster.

"But have you allowed your hate and distrust of your father's invention to blind you to the fact that he is in the very creative process of founding here, in this fertile plateau, a colony of folk, of citizens, who are searching for their rightful place in the Lord's society—seeking an opportunity to share in the bounty of the land and to know the equality of the law?"

"Whether these people will want to remain here permanently, darling, is an open question. But for ourselves, the issue that we face is not social justice, but humanitarianism. We are bound here against our will, and our experience casts doubt on the sincerity of our captors in their urge toward simple justice."

"I too have been numbed by the treatment of those who have sent us here. But we have no recourse other than patience. Your love has been the single beacon on this incredible journey."

"The two of us can surmount any assault on the senses, if not our sensibilities, more so than the band of people who support the Monster for reasons dimly seen. The only way we could suffer, dear, is if, through some occasion, we would lose confidence one with the other."

We embraced again, and hot tears ran down Felicia's

cheeks. "Knowing their intentions is our strongest remedy."

In the way of humanity our tears and sorrow turned to the food in the hamper—fried chicken, cherries, and apples. The meal eaten, I took advantage of the interlude in the zenith of the day to assure Felicia of my love and devotion and to explain once more the fascination of the Monster's complaint. "The only possibility of our escaping this fantasy is to trust each other. Let the claims of those who would cut us asunder be weighed in the scales of justice, in the light of day. Ritter, Mrs. Greene . . . ourselves. We shall prevail."

Felicia clung to me as a child to its mother, and over her bosom I confided, "We shall indeed find a way from here. But resolute measures may still be required. The Monster is simply that. If you keep that in mind, he can be managed. His following, however, is formidable, and he has aims in mind beyond the knowing of our philosophy." I continued, "Something dreadful will happen shortly. I am certain that was the meaning of Ritter's tale, Mrs. Greene's appeal. I know that Greene and the Monster mean us harm."

"Greene, yes," said Felicia. "I know this from the way he glances at me. But not the Monster."

"I disapprove of your nursing the Monster back to health, but perhaps that role can be turned to our advantage. As you learn his habits and overhear talk in his dwelling, we may yet be able to act in time."

"I will come to you every day. If I cannot, I will attempt to send you a message to keep you apprised of my circumstances."

"Prisoners usually are allowed visiting hours, my dear. I am being kept for something special, of that I am certain. Would that I knew what it were. Perhaps the Monster will confide in you."

"I am afraid, Victor. Deadly afraid. I am ashamed that I cannot look upon his countenance without revulsion. Knowing the tale of his treatment of your family fills me with loathing. Yet . . ."

"If you can maintain that feeling, darling, remembering his unprincipled cunning, the way to our freedom is at hand. Somehow we will manage."

We embraced again, standing in the middle of the room. I could feel my passion mount despite the heat and the public nature of our position. But before my throbbing brain could contemplate any further advances, there was a sharp knock on the door. "Time for you to depart, madam." The guard opened the door, and I accompanied Felicia to it. A short distance away William, Greene, and Jenny were visible in serious conversation. Felicia's presence was noted, and Greene beckoned to her. The guard closed the door firmly and shot the bolt, and I was again alone with my wretched cot and the supply stores.

The company of my medical bag, however, was of great satisfaction. In it were still several sources of salvation—the pistol, a bottle of alcohol, and chemicals that could be combined to promote my interests. Yet without a clear plan on what to do with these parts of a possible equation, there was nothing to do but to rest and ponder, rest and ponder, to see how the parts could best be put together. A mistake at this juncture would be my last. That might be tolerable enough, save for Felicia. She was my responsibility, and to see her free of this tribulation was my dearest wish. If only we were both strong enough —strong enough in character, compassion, and love.

There was a sharp thump on the unshuttered window in the back of the long room. Curiosity being one of my brighter characteristics, I investigated. Below the window was a slip of paper with a message, the ultimate in simplicity: "9 J." I pondered only briefly. So Jenny would come that night at nine o'clock and tell me of her problem, which I knew was my problem as well. As I thought about that, I became alert, even excited. I looked forward to the opportunity of knowing her better in all ways, beyond any intelligence that might come my way that dangerous night. The corruption of the place had already seeped into my system.

CHAPTER VII

FLIGHT

My NAP ended about 5 P.M. The jailer entered the depressing room, leaving my supper on the bench—cold roast beef, fresh bread, and two apples, all in all the mark of a generous host. I walked about the storeroom again to get a grip on the reality of my situation before debasing myself on a largesse I had not requested—needed but did not want. I was in a frenzy over my impending meeting with Jenny. Surely her message, and the risk it involved for her, had not been sent simply so we could have another furtive conversation. It had to be of great moment. The question was whether I would be prepared for whatever contingencies might forthwith arise.

The evening air moved easily through the two un-shuttered windows, and, as the heat of the day dissipated, the cool of the night calmed my agitation and my reasoning improved. If there were a prospect for a miracle, it would not come through the iron bars. And as I moved about the storeroom, intrigued by the large barrels of gunpowder, I knew that my release, if that were to be, would come from a novel direction. I turned my head upward and looked carefully over the ceiling, high into the shadows, hoping that a rope would slowly uncoil and provide the means of my elevation from the floor of this dangerous valley.

In a corner of the storeroom was a quantity of old clothing for both sexes. There was a pile of shoes and boots, and somehow it struck me as the place where Greene collected his odd wardrobe. But these were subliminal thoughts. The whole room was sound, and no route of exit was evident.

Then too there was the matter of the guard. Whether he was at the secured door all the time I did not know. Prince, the German shepherd, probably was, however, and from the one close encounter I had had with him, I knew that his skill and vigilance were more to be feared than those of my guard. There was really no way out without removing the dog in some way—a problem that now preoccupied my thoughts.

This concern blended into the prospect of the nine o'clock rendezvous. Would Jenny arrive disguised as a guard and march me off through the ranks of an unsuspecting militia, led by the redoubtable William Digby? Or would her arrival be of a lesser subterfuge, as a patient, to discuss confidentially a female malfunction with a renowned British general practitioner? My mind was not working rationally. My thoughts were disconnected plans, wild fantasies—better, it is true, than insanity or a total mindless acceptance of a situation beyond that bearable by a normal mentality untutored in the mysteries of the origin of life. I tried once again to decide what I should be prepared to do at nine. Finally I concluded that my chance of escaping from the storeroom and the fortress itself—for that is the way I now regarded this rock-escarped plateau—was not going to be any better than this evening. Help in the person of Jenny might be at hand, and if her purpose were otherwise, I still might be able to make my way out simply by her arrival. This variable might work to my advantage. Second, the Monster was still in the process of recovery. This factor was vital, for if he were at the peak of his prowess, his great speed, strength, endurance, and cunning would be decisive to my prospects for a successful escape. There remained the guard and the dog, both of whom would have to be dealt with under any circumstance.

Somehow all this seemed manageable, and I turned to my dinner—and stopped. I saw in the roast beef a possible solution to the dog, uncertain, but possible. I finished the bread and apples. Then I turned my attention to my medical bag. I made up two packets of powders that might in some way smooth my way to freedom—draughts and potions for myself or others. The pistol—should I remove it from its hiding place now and conceal it on my person? If I were determined to leave that evening, then the answer of necessity must be yes. I wavered and felt my resolve slacken. The value of the pistol was always one of surprise, in a setting where the tormentor was unsuspecting and a single pistol shot delivered point blank would splatter the brains like scrambled eggs. But I would take it. I tucked it under my shirt, and the cool muzzle on my stomach reinforced the passion that was growing—the passion to escape.

The decision over the pistol galvanized a series of activities on my part. The pale cast of irresolution lifted and I moved ahead as far as my brain would follow in its logic the steps necessary for me to leave this place. I rolled a blanket, securing in it a canteen of water from my bag, and an oilskin in which I placed jerkin beef from the supply stores. There were quantities of dried foods, as though for a mobile army on the march. I would have taken more—more food, gunpowder, sugar, everything for my own expedition—both out of a desire to deplete their supplies as well as to outfit my own journey, but the exigency for a light load was overwhelming. And there was an incongruity in preparing for a long trip. I would make good quickly or be back in this same room—or worse.

It was eight thirty. The moon, almost full, was already on the eastern edge of the closest range. The mountain looked like a loaf of bread, its lower crust lost in the valleys and rivers below. Now came my first risky maneuver. I scratched at the bar and gave a low whistle, and within seconds there was Prince. He stood below, looking intently into the bars, teeth gleaming white. In that light and angle he looked terrifying and evil, and that rationale made it simpler for me to toss him the roast beef, sprinkled heavily with tasteless arsenic. Yet there was a revulsion as I watched him gulp it down in one massive snap of his powerful jaws, one gnash of his dead-white teeth. My expectation was that he would remove himself from the area within half an hour, an acutely troubled beast. My own conscience was troubled by the ease with which I had taken up the profession of poisoner, as readily as a member of the Borgia clan. It was a weapon of the weak, and I despised myself for using it.

At the door I listened closely for evidence of a guard.

I concluded, reluctantly, that the guard's back was resting solidly on the latched wooden door, and the evenness of the breathing told me that he was asleep. I clicked open my gold pocket watch once more and, in the growing brightness of the moonlight, once again noted the time: two minutes until nine. How might she arrive? On a moonbeam, dancing thro h the bars, or as an angel of the Lord, in dazzling ligut, smiting the guard with a stroke of her righteous sword? I strained my senses for sounds and sights. My keyed-up nerves caused my flesh to twitch at the scuttling sounds of field mice loose among the supplies. Then there was a deeper scratching and a rhythmic thump, thump, thump, barely audible. The very movement of my boots to trace it down eradicated the object of my quest, as the plucking of a wild flower, in that very act, destroys its beauty. Now again it sounded, unmistakably near the base of the wall. I barked my shins against the large trunk on which I had spread my medical wares. It sounded as though someone were inside, a person thrust prematurely into his coffin and now struggling to get out. I was barely able to control my desire to scream out for help—for help from those who would only harm me. Kneeling before the trunk like a savage priest, I at last understood: the quiet, methodical thumping was from beneath the trunk. With great effort I strained and tugged to move one corner of the heavy trunk inch by inch and, by this process, revealed the outline of a small square, cut carefully to conform to the natural timbers of the floor, that, as I stared in the dim light, rose like magic. Below was the face of Jenny, a candle near her chin, summoning me to follow. There was a sharp noise at the door as the guard let his rifle fall. He awoke and shuffled about. The door squeaked. Then he sat down again, yawning. It was quiet, too quiet. Positioning my blanket roll, with the precious oilskin inside, securely over my shoulder, I lowered myself into the small shaft, replaced the lid, and added the thwart that secured it below the floor.

"But they will discover my absence in the morning," I said.

"It will no longer matter," she replied and, crouching, led us on down the underground corridor. The trip ended in no more than fifty yards. Jenny extinguished the candle, and she was gone. I groped around the end of the tunnel and felt my now overexercised state of panic return.

"Up, climb up here, quickly."

There was a dampness like the walls of a cistern, but I scrambled up and into cool air. We were in a small cave in the first ridge west of the storeroom. Jenny was backed against the wall as though she would blend in with it. I followed her example. There was a torchlight at the entrance of the cave, and the voices came directly in, amplified by the silence and the hard and wet sides of the cavern.

"There is still a need for him then?" asked William, the bearer of the torch. The light wavered with the wind and on gusts would cast shadows up to the edge of our hiding place. I thought of leading a retreat to return to the storehouse, but if a single rock rolled about in the process, we would be discovered and trapped like moles in the tunnel of our tomb. Further, from this vantage point we could hear the conversation well, the danger of hearing being no greater than not hearing at all.

"Aye, there is," replied Greene, sitting beyond the torch and out of sight. Yet as he faced the cave, his voice addressed us, as though he were giving a lecture.

"But I understood that once the correct procedure for preparing the fluid was in our hands, there would be no further use for Frankenstein—that he would be of no more value to our plan than this torch."

"Our plan indeed, Digby. My Jenny watched each step and later wrote it down with an eye to every detail. Yet down in the workrooms . . ."

"Something, then, is amiss. Could it be the technicians themselves, sir?" asked William, sensing an irritation in his superior that required a stepping back and down.

"We must know that final step," Greene said. "There must be one element that he somehow concealed from Jenny, something he has kept all to himself. I mean to have it."

"Does the Monster know?"

"No, no, he does not. He plans to extract that information from Frankenstein for himself. He would kill me if he knew what I am trying to do. If we are to have that vital information, then we must have Frankenstein in our exclusive control. But how can we do that without the Monster knowing?"

There was a pause in the conversation. The torch was growing weaker, but the wind still played its tricks. I felt for Jenny's hand and held it. Her grasp was firm. So she had not passed on the correct information—or had she, as had others, simply missed the significance of re-heating the fluid? Had eagerness and greed, or misadventure, or deception, been the agent of this confusion? The general lines of the experimentation were all too well imagined, but the idea of a divergence of purpose, as between the Monster and Greene, and perhaps William, was novel. What kind of society indeed would provide for the diverse aspirations of the ambitious?

"The question is, then, how do we seize him and obtain the information without raising suspicion?"

"We could take him into the forest, squeeze it out of him, and dispose of his body," said William, my manservant of twenty years.

Greene's objections, alas, were not on moral grounds. "The Monster would discover what happened, and God knows his vengeance. He has other plans for the Doctor. But if he were in our hands . . . we might contrive an apparent escape."

"I could, for example, relieve the guard, enter the storeroom, and truss him up," said William, "then bring him out through the secret tunnel here." He pointed up in our direction.

"Or we might enter from the tunnel, drag Frankenstein into it, extract the information, return him, and no one would be the wiser. He would hardly think of reporting his mistreatment to the Monster."

Jenny squeezed my hand tighter. She seemed to sway slightly in my grasp, and my own limbs were beginning to behave improperly. My greatest fear was that the slipperiness of the rocks, oiled by the dripping water, would result in a loud and helpless collapse.

"We have but two more days," said Greene. "If one wanted to challenge the Monster's authority now, perhaps it could be done. Yet Ritter and his flock are devoted to him, and if something were to happen adverse to his interests, their vengeance would be thorough."

"The timing remains vital," said William. "The Duke of Wellington had time on his side, whereas Napoleon did not."

"You are in charge of the militia, Digby," said Greene curtly, "but I am in command of the strategy. I must do what must be done. The enterprise is too promising for quarreling, yet the future will be decided now. So we have these contradictions that must be resolved."

"Then as to Frankenstein . . ." The wind whirled the dead leaves and the torch flared briefly, sending the fingers of light up along the wall of the cave like so many crawling spiders. My boots began to slip out from under me, and I held on to Jenny with my left hand and felt my right palm begin to slide down the wall. I pressed it harder into the rock, and I could feel its sharp edges cutting into the thick of the palm. For the moment fear acted as an anesthesia.

"We will have to act decisively," said Greene, "for he is still the prize, the apple. Once we have our bite, we can dispose of the core, the seeds, the pit, and the stem."

I was slowly sinking on my left leg as my right boot steadily reached out into the dankness of the cave. My thigh muscles tightened, and my right palm would have wept had it had another biological fate. Jenny held my left hand, but her strength was draining.

"What am I to do?" asked William.

"Tomorrow night meet me here at nine and we will do as required."

The torch moved away from the entrance and back toward the storehouse. I slumped against the floor of the cave, in pain and mental exhaustion. Stones rattled down toward the entrance. It was Jenny who would not let me rest.

"You have heard what they said. There is no time to dissipate. Let me show you the way."

I followed her brisk pace on a trail leading on over the first ridge, down into a narrow valley with a dry stream bed. There were enough of these streams in the Downs so that I could not tell where they led, except in their general direction off to the north and east. High on the far bank were two native craft, canoes of sorts, stranded by the retreat of the waters. They were probably used as ferries or fishing crafts in normal water levels. We walked along this way for perhaps an hour. The moon climbed ever higher, and the great bright stars dotted the heavens. The shadows of the ridges narrowed as the moon neared its zenith. At last we stopped, and sat, exhausted, in the dry pine blanket halfway up the last ridge before the outer barricade, which rose straight up, or so it seemed, with the natural outcroppings of the stone fortress walls for the final 500 feet. I unrolled my blanket, opened the canteen, and then took from the oilskin the small packet of jerkin beef. She drank greedily, but declined the food.

"There is little time, Doctor," she said, trying to compose her mind and her thoughts. "I have acted impulsively, and I have found in the past that my impulses are not my most reliable guide."

"That is true," I nodded, my own sins fresh upon me. My early meetings with Greene, my attempt to poison the Monster, my violation of Felicia . . . My God, Felicia. My mind had not once been set in her direction for the whole afternoon and evening, so intent had I been in thinking of my own welfare. I became somber, even morose, and Jenny sensed that her opening statement had struck home in ways she had not contemplated.

"I have lived a difficult life," she continued, "and before it is too late, I wish to set things straight, whatever their outcome on my future happiness."

Her story of a humble life, coming from a background of poverty and debauchery, was one familiar to me from the daily observations of the slums of London. Her employment as a serving girl in the Dolphin Bar and her subsequent meeting with Greene prepared the way for her marriage and training as a nurse. "Frederick at that time seemed like a saint, one who was sent from heaven to raise me from my bondage and to make life meaningful."

"And this was not the outcome?" I asked.

Her face was downcast, and her beauty was accentuated by the diffusion of the moonlight into our pine bower. "Frederick returned home one night over a year ago in a frenzy of excitement. He would tell me nothing of the reason, but he began to have delusions of power, a determination to dominate me and everyone else. His great energy and determination are wholly committed to this mad scheme that will be played out on this pasture. I am terrified of him. You understand as I do his coarseness of character and his insensitivity to human values. He was not always this way. Now he is among the victims of his own design."

"I have talked to the Reverend Ritter, but I did not understand him to allude to anything other than certain spiritual expectations."

"Yes, that too, but that is only the means to a greater

and more ambitious end. Greene and his new man, William Digby, well known to you, are talking of new social experiments, a social order that will be superior to anything yet known to man. They aspire for a kind of state within a state, an enclave in this wild place where their strength and accomplishments will swell their area of control in ever-increasing circles."

"And the Monster?"

"He is the author of the plan, truth to tell. But I fear that the ending is still much in doubt."

"Are not Greene and William playing an exceedingly dangerous game?"

"I am no longer worried about the danger of their plans, or those of the Monster. The scheme itself is a hideous thing, and its success depends on the duping of the innocent and the blood of the living and the dead. It must be stopped."

"But how?" I asked. "What can be done?"

"I have not helped you this far simply to save you, although I cannot account for what you may make of this opportunity, if it is successful. You must succeed in leaving this colony, this valley of evil, and alert the authorities. They must come here in force and put an end to the whole matter, drive a stake in the heart of this unholy place."

Jenny trembled and shook as her sense of outrage rose as well as her feelings for this valley spread so peacefully under heaven. "Your escaping will do two things," she continued, laying her hand on my brow as I stretched out on the dusty needles. "First, the process of quickening the dead will not proceed. They simply do not know how to make the fluid, and without that their other efforts, elaborate as they are, will not succeed."

"But you know."

"I do, that is true, but only you are aware that I know it."

"Does not concealing that fact place my life in grave jeopardy?"

"It does, as you heard, but because of that burden, I have felt compelled to help you. A further delay may start the breakup of this uneasy alliance in itself. But beyond that, your escape will accelerate that possibility. They will quarrel over who is responsible, and they will worry that you will expose them."

"What will they do?"

"I do not know. But they will not do what they are now doing." She continued to soothe my brow and then, to my surprise, kissed me quietly and for a long moment on my forehead.

"And if I do not go on?" I asked. My blood was turning cold over the prospect for Felicia, expressly held as a guarantee of my co-operation.

"I rely on your sense of right and wrong, of good and evil, as a man of sensibility, someone whose life has been touched by this mad desire to do things beyond the limits of heaven and earth, to know that it is evil and must be stopped."

"But if I am missed, will they not redouble their efforts to carry out their plans and to move before whatever effort the authorities may make can be implemented?"

"They cannot proceed without you," she said calmly.

I sat back up and looked toward the ridge line. The moon was half concealed, and against the glowing silver disk was the outline of pines and spruce, feathered in their tips, holding dark and impenetrable secrets in their boughs and branches. This was not so simple a matter as she outlined. The authorities might or might not respond to my tale, and once again, as it had plagued my father, there was the question of responsibility for the slaughter that might be unleashed on this community by my father's creation, so skillfully rejuvenated by me. And in my flight, what of the prospect of finding the notebooks, the secret of life? This was a prize indeed. And what if my escape was no more than a ruse on the part of the beautiful Jenny to become the vital link in the chain, in a kind of alliance with the Monster at the expense of her ambitious husband and the pompous William Digby? These dark thoughts joined forces with the cicadas and the whippoorwills, and the bats that circled through the pines in their quest for sustenance. Life is hard without trust, but if you do not give it, neither shall you receive it.

"You are taking a grave risk in releasing me," I said instead. "I should think Greene would murder you for less."

"Frederick loves me, Frankenstein, and I have nothing to fear from him."

"But . . ."

"You do not understand love, Doctor." She placed her arms about my neck and drew me to her. The fire inside her spread to me, and we found each other inside our bower. "I want your seed, Frankenstein, for this night I feel fertile. I want your seed, to take with me far away, and to reassemble the life that I thought I had but that has become a cruel illusion."

As we lay together on my blanket, spent, the juices of love warm on our genitals, our eyes looked up to the loveliness of the moon—and then froze. Along the ridge line, moving fast and without noise, probably because of the contrary direction of the light evening breeze, was the Monster, rampant. And behind him, knee high, was Prince. They were not fifty yards away, and had it not been for the arsenic that must have had a sickening effect on the German shepherd, surely he would have winded us, the smell of love alone enough to have him bound on down the mountain, with the Monster but a pace behind.

Neither of us spoke for at least five minutes, and when we resumed our conversation, detumescence had set in. It was not until we had both readjusted our clothing and I had rolled up the blanket into its simple pack that my hands stopped shaking. "What chance do you think I have of making good my escape?"

Jenny looked solemn and tired and beaten. "I had not thought he would recover so soon. This was why I wanted to have you off as soon as possible, to preclude such a development."

"Do you think he is searching for me?"

"Perhaps. Although he is more a creature of the night than the day, because of his treatment by humanity in general. He savors the night, which hides his features and increases his powers over any human competition."

"If the alarm has not yet been raised, the guard will certainly know of my disappearance around six or so, and the alarm will then be sounded. But if the Monster is simply enjoying his new strength, he may well sleep into the morning, and so if I get under way, I may be able to reach the top of the rock wall in the early morning and make good my escape."

"The climb will be difficult, but there is no other way."

I held her again. I would do as she asked. What else could I do, and what more could I expect from her to prove her earnestness about my well-being and the sincerity of her concern over the fate of the valley?

"What will you do?" I asked.

"I will return to my cabin. My husband will be in those gloomy caves the whole night. I do not think he will have reason to seek me out until dawn. It was of course a risk to come out here, but it is something I had to do. I am above all drawn to you. It was a risk well worth taking."

"There are some things I would have you do for me," I said. "First, here is my own pistol. I wish you would securely pass it on to Felicia, for whatever eventually may come her way. And here are two packets of potions, with written instructions for use. She is to know that her safety is uppermost in my mind." I wanted to add more, about love, but the lack of appropriateness was more than I could bear. My own feelings about Jenny were confused. Did I love her as well? "Finally, you must say something to Ritter, so that he will know I have not abandoned him and his hopes. I . . ."

"No, do not say that. Don't say that if this evil is abolished, the disease will linger in you and once again wreak its toll."

The vehemence of her tone underlined the depth of concern she had already expressed on this whole subject, yet I thought that some reassurance on my part to Ritter was needed.

"Will you simply tell him that I am thinking of him, then?" I said.

"If it is important to you, I will say that but no more. There too is a risk, because of his personal habits. He might say something indiscreet to Frederick so he would understand that it was I who was the instrument of your release."

"I think there is more of a risk to his group and himself if he grows discouraged and presses on for his Resurrection Day, as he calls it. That is a moment no one should be called upon to face."

Jenny nodded and squeezed my arm. I wanted to ask more about what was taking place in the workhouses in the caves. She knew more, a good deal more, but the hour was late, past midnight, and I had a long way to go.

"I have a happy feeling about this night," I said, holding her to me again. "I have come to know you and to understand you, and the risk you are taking and the cogency of your plan are both inspirations to me. I will somehow scale that cliff and return with assistance. I do not see how they can proceed without me, unless they finally suspect and turn on you. You are in grave danger yourself, and I urge you to do nothing more than that to which we have agreed."

"One final thing," she said. "Take one of my mother-of-pearl hairpins. At the Berkeley Springs Inn there is a Mrs. Comstock, who is the cook. She is a long-time friend. She will know this pin and vouch for my reliability in your conversation with the Captain of the Militia. This may help spur him to move quickly."

I took the hairpin and placed it in my jacket pocket. Had I a token I would have given it to her as a keepsake of our understanding, something beyond that which might be easing toward her womb. Instead, I had given her my pistol for delivery to another—a death sentence by Greene if he found it on her person. Dangerous for Felicia too, but somehow, there were more pluses than losses in this. "If you have need of the pistol before it is delivered, do not hesitate to use it."

"I will not use it, Doctor. The person for whom it is intended has the greater need. Her situation will be truly parlous on the morrow when those evil men discover your disappearance."

"If I do not succeed, it will all have been in vain. But I must go."

We embraced again in our bower, our place in this very wide world, this tiny private place where for one moment our fears and apprehensions had been suspended and we had laid open our souls to each other. True, I did not tell her of my deepest suspicion, as unworthy—that she would use her knowledge of the making of the formula to control the group. She disappeared within a moment down the trail, and I started up toward the ridge where the Monster had passed. I moved slowly and carefully to avoid any unnecessary noise. What if he were to come back?

At the top of the ridge, I lay down on the pine-needle-covered ground and slowly worked across the twenty yards until the moonlight would not silhouette me against the black and star-strewn sky. A surge of energy was following this taste of physical danger and excitement—too soon, I feared, for I would need the extra strength more on the morrow than now when the climbing, despite the dark, was relatively easy. Every few paces, however, I paused and listened intently for any sound that might indicate that the Monster and Prince were in the area. It was extraordinary that he had chosen this ridge at this time to show his recovery. Had he known that I was there, and if so, how would he have found out? Had someone followed us from the cave? If they had, and then had alerted him, he could easily have overtaken us.

At the top of the last ridge before the descent into the valley and then the climb of perhaps 1,500 feet, the last 500 feet sheer rock and almost vertical, I could see, two ridges over, a series of torches crossing, as though a group were moving through the forest. Pursuit! In an hour they would be at my ridge, while I would be lost to their view on the forested slope of the rock wall. Then for those last 500 feet I would be visible like an ant on a ceiling, making my way across those exposed rocks. They would have to capture me, if what Jenny said was correct, so that would be in my favor. If they changed their minds, I would be well out of range of rifle fire from this ridge, and if they followed from below I was at least one hour ahead of them. This meant that I had to climb that exposed 500 feet in no more than one hour. Once over the top, I would head directly east and should find succor from humanity in general, something that did not exist within the crenelated confines of this moody valley.

My sense of mission was impaired by my feeling that, in the Armageddon that might result from the meeting of the authorities and the Monster, the notebooks of my dear father would be forever lost. I was their rightful heir and I was confident that, through the searing experience I had already encountered, I would be a worthy keeper of the gates. I wanted that power, however, and I would have it. Also, psychically, I was out of tune with myself, the experience with Jenny being so immediate and overwhelming that my troth to Felicia seemed unreal and a long time ago, something that had happened elsewhere in a different time and age. My act of unfaithfulness, for I knew no other word for it, depressed and saddened me as much as it had exhilarated me at the time. Felicia would understand, I was certain, why I had behaved as I did and why it did not affect our love; she would realize that my intentions toward her were, and always had been, the most honorable and loving. Nothing that Jenny or I had done or said would blemish our betrothal. Felicia would be forgiving if I told her, but on the other hand, her forgiveness might well be large enough to forgo the telling.

I picked up my pace on the downhill side, bobbing and weaving from side to side to increase my acceleration safely. I was noisier than I would have liked, but the danger of delay was certain, with the pursuers not an hour behind, while the chance of running into the Monster was more remote. Or was it? Was it possible that he was ahead of his pack of jackals and would snatch me up just as success seemed almost certain?

There was no point in including such thoughts in my overburdened brain. The climb up through the oaks and maples was well under way by four o'clock. If I had not been so tired, the climb at about 60 degrees would have been faster. In the pines and spruces the angle of ascent rose and the outcroppings of shale rock became more frequent. At dawn I was at the rock edge, and five hundred feet above, almost straight up, was the crown of my efforts. I abandoned the blanket roll, placing the oilskin in my jacket pocket. Low clouds were hanging over the face of the cliff, and it was cool and shadowy as I made my way out and up on the bare rock face. There were fairly simple ridges, the first diagonal leading a third of the way up; and by standing vertically and keeping a light touch on the face, I got off to a good start. But at the end of the traverse, the situation became more difficult. The shale crumbled here and there under my boots, and I began to cling closer and closer to the wall. A downward glance brought on acute vertigo, and I hung like a bee to a flower for several minutes until my head cleared. It was almost five miles back to the valley settlement. They might well be watching through telescopes. But I was almost out of their reach, and with that thought I continued to climb up out of the shadows, toward the top and freedom and sanity. Such a short and happy thought.

CHAPTER VIII

CAPTURED

I was two hundred feet up the face of the cliff. It was both more difficult and simpler than I had imagined from a distance. There were places where footholds seemed to disappear as in a stretch of sand in the desert. There were, however, more straggly, but strong, shrubs to cling to than I had expected, and the diagonal shale produced comfortable stretches of path that were surprisingly easy to traverse. But it was those bleak and dangerous distances between the shale paths that taxed my strength and ingenuity. I approached the shale foot by foot and tried not to think of the fact that I had now worked my way halfway to the top. Going back appeared to be more difficult than going forward, and my mind concentrated on accomplishing the latter objective—except when it wandered. I wondered about Jenny, whether she had gotten back safely, escaping the pursuers and any contretemps with Greene in case he learned of her absence. I also wondered who was leading the chase after me, and who was being blamed for my escape. But these thoughts evaporated at the sight of the rock ledge I now faced. I had seen this ledge earlier but had ignored the implications, as I was learning to do with my problems. It was nothing more than a shadow at first. The clouds were still with me, a damp and pleasant mist, not enough to make the rocks slippery but promising rain sometime ahead. Then behind the clouds, like a candle lighted in the dusk and growing bright in the dark of evening, there came the sun. The mist progressively lightened, and in the time that it took me to decide on a new hand hold and another step up the almost vertical slope, the sun burst through. The clouds raced away like truant children.

I felt suddenly like an actor in the center of a stage. The eye of whomever was upon me, and I was naked to his glance. My pursuers were still half an hour away, far enough for me to make good my escape and leave them sniffing on these very rocks, undecided where to go or what to do. But the Monster. If he had joined or was leading the chase, then what? I remembered the scene again at Mont Salève, the sketch of his fantastic ascent up that mountain overlooking Geneva. His proclivity for the mountains, the sheer walls, might, in fact, have been inspired by the ease of his ability to climb. The idea was grotesque, a being eight feet high and fifteen stone bolting up the side of a mountain. What power and skill to thrust up and up, hanging independent of the laws of gravity! And why not? Such laws of physics were naught to violate if one considered first his total disregard of the universe. If right was wrong, then up might as well be down. But there was no sound, no call of that dreaded voice. And in that silence there was a powerful inner urging of my own: make sure of the final one hundred feet.

It was my fear of falling that slowed my progress. The more success I had on this rocky face, the more fear I had that each attainment would be my last. I had inched my way back to the left, above the vertical and diagonal ridge that had brought me up to my early success. Here at last I was just below the shale ledge that had cast gloom across the outer recesses of my brain, the sentinels that see in the night, that edge of consciousness that wakes and soothes, confident that the trouble will disappear of its own volition. This ledge was a greater problem than I could possibly have thought. By the time my tenuous trail reached it, my head bumping on its underside, the ledge extended out two feet from the wall of the cliff. If I could somehow follow it off to my right, there was a place fifteen feet away where the lip of the ledge was no more than one foot, with footholds and shrubs that would allow me to hoist myself upon it and then march on further to the right to the last series of small but workable holds that would launch me to the top. But there was no way to make those fifteen feet.

An experienced Alpine guide would have taken this ledge into his plan of ascent, pausing little more than to place his ax in a crack and lever himself onto the ledge. But I had no ax, and even if I did, no experience on how to hoist myself up and over the ledge. I finally grasped it firmly with both hands and then, pressing out and up, moved my feet, one after the other, up the slope, placing my left forearm on the top of the ledge and trying to follow with my left leg and pull myself on up to safety. My boots had worn and were slippery to the touch of the side of the wall; and, as I tried to slip up and over the rock, my right boot slipped on the shale, and I began to slide back under the ledge, my weight now suspended by a throbbing left arm. I was desperate to regain a purchase with my right foot. I reinforced my grasp of the ledge with my right hand, but with so little leverage left, I could see no prospect for myself but an effort to find my way back to my foothold against the wall. My head was bowed and bruised by the wall of the ledge, but my immediate interest was in regrouping my four limbs so that a fresh assault on the ledge would be possible. My failing right foot, sliding again and again along the face of the rock without finding any relief, was jeopardizing my entire ascent. I at last hung on with both arms and swung into the cliff, finding temporary relief in a narrow shelf, which still left me clinging by my hands to the ledge and my body suspended into the emptiness of the airy void. My hope was to swing my body like a pendulum and at the precise moment pull and twist myself onto the top of the ledge and cling there like a swamp leech.

At that very moment, when I was straining with all my might to swing over the ledge, there was a great disturbance off to my right and almost at the top of the cliff, followed by a numbing explosion, a whistle of crumping sounds, then a slow slide of earth and rocks, gathering momentum down the side of the cliff. Ducking back under the ledge, I gasped as this great avalanche of earth and stones showered past me in a mighty rumble, so strong that at last I could hold on no longer and fell into the trailing end of this massive slide. As I went on down in a curious sense of falling and sliding, of terror and of repose, I recognized what had happened: an artillery shell had dislodged me from my climb. So William Digby, gimpy castoff of the field artillery, had had his day. The idea that the forces of the Monster had artillery was not one that was foremost in my concerns as I went on down toward the approaching trees in a choking dust, a torrent of rocks and shrubs ever before me, and then the impact of the body with the first line of pines. I was stunned as I fell and overwhelmed by a sense of failure and fatality, the conviction that as one individual I could make no more difference in this scheme of events than the rocks that bore me down.

My return to consciousness was similar to the sensation in my many dreams of falling. A feeling of coldness and pressure around the forehead, a whirl of disjointed scenes, and then the voice, "Are you all right, Doctor?"

I wanted to respond; I wanted to cry out that it was dangerous for one man to fire at another with a cannon— that my desire to leave on my own was a personal whim and unconnected to any general desire to refuse my support to works of Christian charity.

No answer came from my lips, although things to say were now revolving in my brain at an ever-increasing rate, like the speed of a carriage. I could hear and see, but for the nonce, I could not speak. When I say "see," my sight was not perfect. The person hovering over me spun, and in that whirlpool I could see a familiar black hat. It went round and round and then stopped. I gasped with fear.

"Be not afraid, Frankenstein. I will help you." It was the Reverend Ritter. He was clear-eyed, his face determined. In the background were several of his congregation, good men and true, and, more important, armed with rifles. He raised me up in his arms, and a follower touched his canteen to my dusty lips.

"It was God's love, a miracle that brought you down that mountain alive," said Ritter. He removed his hat, bowed his head, folded his hands one onto the other, and, lips moving, prayed to God for my relief. It was one prayer that was quickly answered. I could not believe my good fortune on having fallen down the vertical side of that mountain onto the wooded slopes with no more injury than bruises and scratches. I was indeed a child of God, who, at that moment, unconcerned with sparrows that fall, had placed his divine hand in my path and delivered me, like an infant, into the arms of the Reverend Ritter.

"What am I to do?" I asked him. "I have failed in my task and am, for all practical concerns, once again a prisoner."

"You are not a prisoner, Frankenstein, but an ally. Once I learned of your escape and of the determination of Greene to reclaim you at whatever cost, I moved to save you. I have arrived in time, but time is precious. Greene's men will be here soon. Listen! I hear the sound of dogs." Far over the ridge toward the settlement came the nervous barking of dogs on the trail. I thought I heard the voice of Prince, but I did not dwell on that.

"But where are we to go? What are we to do? We are all trapped by the same evil forces. Artillery, in Digby's hands! God knows what will be the aspirations of these unprincipled men."

"Rise, Frankenstein—rise and we will move off. We will seize the moment, returning to the settlement while our enemies circle these parts for your person or your remains."

The last hazard I had anticipated was an artillery

round. True, it had struck the cliff a hundred yards away. One could conjecture that the aim had not been to destroy me but to retrieve me, if Jenny had been correct. On the other hand, at a range of five miles, who could say what was the intent, whether the round had been long or short, left or right? Jenny might even have suggested the attack, wanting the secret of the fluid to herself and the power over this macabre project. "I obey your wishes, Reverend, but if it is possible during the return, I wish to learn the present circumstances and what your private views are at this juncture."

Ritter was all alertness and led a fast traverse across the lower base of the cliff, concealed by the pines, on down a dry stream bed, and then through another creek of spring water in an effort to obscure our route from our pursuers, whose dogs were sounding closer and more excited by the minute. It was over an hour, when again we found a small creek and followed it, before Ritter risked a brief halt. He posted the scouts about the resting place. He was in great agitation, visible in the flashing of his eyes and the jut of his jaw. "Frankenstein, I must know what is in store for my children and myself. Since our talk, I have had grave misgivings about the course I have taken. The Monster has denied his presence from me on the grounds of his weakness and convalescence. Yet when I sought him out, he was gone, like Christ from the tomb, and your lady, Felicia, was mystified as to what had happened. Her sense of puzzlement and fear, good doctor, only matched my own."

"And when did you see her?" I asked excitedly.

"Late in the evening, when I thought surely the Monster would be in repose and would speak to me. I need his reassurance, Frankenstein, and it is not forth-coming from his supporters, the cruel Greene and the arrogant Digby. My patience grows short, and if my aid and patience are not soon rewarded, the sword of the Lord shall be made known in these parts. No goodness and mercy shall follow the paths of those who have deceived me."

"Of the possibility of deception, my dear Ritter, I have long suspected. But is there proof?"

Ritter shuddered. "My faith and that of my followers will overcome your misgivings, Frankenstein; yet, saying that, I must know. I must know for certain. I would lead you now to a hidden entrance of the very cave so that you can see for yourself and report thereupon to me. I hold myself back, out of God-given fear and confidence, if you will, but be assured that if the progress is not as I have bargained for, the hand of vengeance shall not be forestalled."

I would have talked longer, but the restless and determined Ritter was on his feet, and we again moved swiftly through the unmarked forest, guided as by a divine light. Within another two hours of steady downhill marching, we came to the final ridge wherein were hidden the Monster's laboratories. We were again at the crossing of the stream, the two wooden boats, high and dry, the strewn boulders at the edge of the rocky boar's back of a ridge.

"I will leave you at this hidden entry," Ritter said. "It is safe enough here. The nearest guards are usually asleep in the sentry box, at least a hundred yards downstream at a confluence. With God's help, you should return in three hours—with the truth. I require the truth."

The entry he referred to was not apparent to the untutored eye. First of all, there were none of the ubiquitous guards that surrounded the other side of the hill. If there were guards downstream at a sentry box, so much the better. One assumed that most of the guard personnel were committed to the village side, where the obvious curiosity seekers roamed. No one was allowed on that side of the ridge. This was the blind side, where there was no reason to expect visitors, welcome or not. But Ritter in his wanderings had learned of this entry. If one looked more closely, there was a series of metal rods aimed at the heavens and disappearing into the cracks and crevices of the earth. There was a draft of cool air from the subterranean depths. It was as black inside as a bat and as silent as a pine cone.

"I understand your desire to know, Reverend, but why do you make me your chosen instrument?"

He drew closer, his eyes burning and his unshaven face unbearably close. "Whom else can I rely upon? If one of my own discovered treachery, he would try to resolve the matter then and there, a guarantee of greater tragedies."

Ritter had thought through the problems further than I had. So I was brief. "I will go as you say. But in turn, you must pattern your behavior on the normal pace of activity and give no hint, not the slightest indication of discontent. For I have a foreboding that dark forces are in conflict. Our own lives can be vouchsafed only by calm and courage. I hope I am not lacking on both counts."

I pondered on whether to say more to Ritter about Jenny, whether to explain the assets of the pistol and the potions to this man of God, or a man who would be God. His status raised my apprehension, whichever way it was resolved. I considered telling Ritter my own thoughts, having as it were a feeling that if somehow our side could muster its hidden strength, all these outrageous wrongs might be righted. Yet to coalesce these forces prematurely, while the various opponents of the settled way of the world were at their zenith, would be to destroy them. So I concluded simply, "Pray for me, Reverend, and give my love to Felicia."

"I will surely do both," he said. "I am worried about the ability—yes, and the intention—of the Monster and his men to make good their promise. Yet I must temper my misgiving with belief in the Father, the Son, and the Holy Ghost. Even a simple stool must have at least three legs; otherwise it will not stand." So saying, he walked off, a pocket Bible clutched to his breast and his eyes toward heaven. The armed followers fell into place behind him and set off for the nearby settlement.

Alone, I looked about me. There was no one visible. I looked again at the hole before me. It was small and deep and reminded me of the grave. It was with difficulty and apprehension that I lowered myself into it, feeling that I was simplifying the task of my enemies and losing myself from the serious pursuit of justice. Yet mesmerized and forever hopeful, a trait I had somehow received from Aunt Margaret, I descended into this opening of the earth. It was simpler to go down than to go up.

The coolness of the descent, with the promise of even more relief, raised my spirits and increased my ability to crawl like a worm through this tiny crevice. It was a natural entry, not carved by man, and for that reason it was tight and difficult. Although it began to widen somewhat, I feared that I would be caught in the narrow passages like a rodent and die a gruesome death, held fast by the rocks and secured by the iron laws of gravity. Yet down and down I went, with a small shower of earth and stone. As I gasped for breath, I slipped out onto a vaulted walk, a natural cave of impressive dimensions, the stalactites hanging down like so many threatening swords. Aside from the trickle of water and the faint rushing sound of a stream, there was silence. I feared the silence. I had been too much with myself for endless days to welcome the sound of nothingness. I could not cope with it. To relieve the silence, I wanted to cry out, to demand my right as a human being to be associated with mankind. It was with great difficulty that I moved forward up the grade, where my instinct told me my fellow man would be found. That expectation proved to be the most cruel in my memory; but if one knew what lies ahead, who among us would not retreat?

The grade started down again, until I felt it might well be below the level of the surrounding plateau. There were side paths leading off both higher and lower, but the main path was clear enough. There was now a humming sound, which on a happier occasion I might have attributed to bees. And there were bats, passing quietly in the corridor on their way to rest until the night. What ghastly machinations would I find to report to Ritter, and then what would be the outcome? The balance of forces on the Downs confused me. Where I had expected unity and organization, I had instead found factions and rancor. The single strand that held the web together, these people of diverse objectives, was the promise of the

Monster to create life, to raise the dead, to quicken the clay. In that was the power and the glory, and the actors all instinctively knew it—I among them, who had no other purpose now in life than to reclaim my heritage.

These dreary and elevating thoughts were interrupted, however, by the end of the path. Before me was a massive door made of split pine logs bound together crudely but strongly with iron crossties and massive hinges. The door was at least eight feet tall and four feet wide. There was no handle on my side. It seemed to be a construction barrier, a sealing off of the chamber beyond, rather than an opening into the interior. And all the while the humming sound was more intense. I felt the door carefully, for the dim light from the openings high in the ceiling provided only the roughest delineations of light from dark, although my eyes had adjusted satisfactorily to the half-light of this underworld.

There was no choice but to retrace my steps until I found a smaller trail, and I chose one that made off to the right and higher in the cave. I was soon on my hands and knees, and the drippings of the stalactites smelled salty and gave me the impression of acid that would, in time, be devastating to clothing and flesh. Yet I went on in a partial frenzy, knowing not what else I could do. With my fortune at such an impasse, I was not prepared to see light ahead, dim, but nonetheless the evidence of man's hand, the Promethean torch that has for so long bedeviled its possessors. On my stomach I reached an opening, and there, spread out into the gloom, were the outer reaches of the Monster's laboratories.

Charnel house would be the proper word. Yet the absence of an overwhelming odor that one associates with

flesh in various stages of decomposition indicated a so-
phisticated undertaking. The character of the atmosphere
in the cave was remarkable in terms of preservation.
There was the unmistakable cool airiness of the place
that I had not associated with such underground caverns,
despite the occasional pools from the stalactites. There
were open tubs, massively built of timber and secured
by iron, filled with the carcasses of animals. I could recognize the anatomical parts of deer and bear, for example,
and, as I had expected, human beings. They seemed to
be in a state of preservation—a natural preservation, for
I assumed a later and more complicated processing, ac-
cording to my father's notebooks. These were the materials, as bricks for a house, to be assembled in whatever way into the beings the Monster would construct.
Surely not he himself. The idea was too grotesque.
But he must have assembled a team for this purpose
which had been engaged for many months in this un-
earthly affair. There was no one visible in this vast chamber. My curiosity outweighed my fear and disgust, and
I slipped down the rock wall slowly, breaking my fall
by hand holds and scuffing boots. Could I scale that wall
on my return? I looked slowly about. The chamber was
more than fifteen feet high and forty feet in either direction. The tubs were grisly reminders of the work at
hand.

The humming sound increased, as did the rhythm
of the rushing water. I walked quickly by the tubs to the
far end of the chamber. The door here was of no less
massive size than the first door I had seen, but it was
slightly ajar. Feeling like Jack in the tale of the bean-
stalk, I pushed open the door and found myself in a

room of similar proportions, but with a series of sturdy wooden tables like oversized butcher blocks. There lay, in various stages of completion, a series of potential beings. They were all of outlandish size, like the Monster himself, leading me to consider that there was some logical reason for such a figure other than sheer terror. This would seem to be a crude process, with the finishing work, the careful sewing and suturing, in the hands of others further along the line. It was clear, though, in the dim light of the oil lamps, that this was an amalgam of flesh and parts, and that the Reverend Ritter's hope for his flock had been misplaced. There was yet another door, and that too proved to be open.

I entered the next chamber with more caution. My fortune so far had made me overbold, and the sights themselves had reduced my mind to a simple single cell that reacted only to light and darkness. Here there were three lines of tables, plain sheets covering the objects that lay beneath. The humming sound I now recognized, for along the far wall ran an underground stream, which turned a small water wheel. A long row of crude electric cells generated current supplied by the metal rods and chemicals. The gauges on galvanometers registered the voltage, and wires from the electric cells were attached in negative and positive poles to the objects on the table. Electricity and the fluid, then, were the essence of life. Not life—animation. Life as I knew it had a spiritual and moral quality absent in the Monster. The hand of God touched not on this ghastly enterprise.

Just as I was in position to lift the sheet to complete my investigation and report with certitude to Ritter on the fate of his flock, out of the shadow stepped a familiar figure, the shadow of his round hat exaggerated by the light he blocked from the table.

"I have waited patiently for you, Frankenstein. And you came when you were needed."

I drew back from the table to flee, until I saw in a converging circle Greene's motley armed guards. But in the country of the blind, these warriors were supreme. "Come with me," Greene ordered in his hard-toned voice, "and I will discuss with you my requirements . . . and strike, if possible, a satisfactory bargain."

Greene ordered me through another well-built door and into a storeroom, where he led me to two chairs beside a table. An exceptionally large candle burning on the table revealed in the background kegs and cases, military supplies, the armament for this mad enterprise. Greene's pistol was in evidence in his belt. He did not remove it to threaten me, but I knew that any resistance on my part would bring his beggars to the rescue.

"I will come to the point, Frankenstein. I demand the explanation of the formula for the fluid."

It was incredible to me that he had not already learned it, from Jenny in the first instance before she had reason to withhold the information. Had Greene not placed her by my side for that very purpose? Or in the burden of the work had this somehow escaped her agile mind? No, she had indicated that she understood. I had no right to my suspicion.

"It is impossible for you, Greene, to understand the tragedy that the knowledge of this unnatural process has already wreaked. Cease in this unholy effort while you still have your health and sanity."

Greene's rage surged within him and his breathing

quickened. Then he became calm, the coolness of the
serpent, so it seemed to me. "Think not, Frankenstein,
that all the suffering of this world has taken place solely
in your breast. I have already suffered much—so much, in
fact, that there is no rationale for what has been done
unless this project sees its way to fruition."

"My answer is no."

Greene was prepared for this. "Knowing what this
means to me, I will not easily be thwarted. And only then
if your life and those of your loved ones mean nothing
to you." He removed his pistol and thumped the butt
firmly on the table. Two guards appeared in a twinkling.
I was bound hand and foot and securely tied to the heavy
chair.

Greene placed his delicate stiletto on the table, a
knife that showed the cunning and degeneration of his
brain, for of what use was such a knife to an honest man?
"You and your loved ones." I pondered that. Whom could
he mean? In lying to myself, my face flushed. Had he
found out about the previous evening with Jenny? Would
she betray me so easily? Why had he not said "loved one,"
simply indicating Felicia? Why had I not seen the evil,
the cruel and perverse streak, in Greene when I first
set eyes on him? But how different his aspect in the civilized setting of dear Aunt Margaret's library than in his
natural environment. His gloomy features were in keeping with the shades and shadows of the underground, as
was his odd clothing snatched from the bodies of the dead.

"I had at first thought of bringing your lady to this
place and torturing her until you weakened to the point
of co-operation. Yet there will be punishment enough
left for her if she simply stays on here by herself, I sus-

pect. And from what I have observed, yours is a selfish nature and no drop of blood anywhere, even the Lamb's blood, means as much to you as your own." He fingered the knife with affection. "It is useless for you to resist, Frankenstein. And it is only through me that you may have an opportunity to lead your former life of privilege."

"What, then, is your offer, although no man of honor would take advantage of the disparity in our freedom in striking a fair bargain."

"The fluid—first of all the fluid. But then, in the aftermath, assuming your desire to return to England, an opportunity to do so."

"My freedom is under the guarantee of the Monster himself," I responded.

"Which is worth nothing if the Monster chooses to ignore it," Greene added softly, "or if he does not have the final strength to ensure it."

"You find the Monster in the way of your own ambitions?"

"I speak frankly," said Greene, "because you will not carry tales. His hatred of mankind is so obsessive that I see no way to assume, less to assure, that he will not turn against any human being, friend or foe. We have so far been working toward the same end of extending our power, through the creation of forces that are susceptible to our will. But once these new forces are created, whether they will be used for good or evil depends on their master. And no man can serve two masters," concluded Greene with his particularly offensive laugh, a silent, mocking laugh.

"What good works really are you up to?"

"I have a sincere and deep feeling for the oppressed,

for the disadvantaged. We are exploited daily by the lumber interests, the mine interests, all taking the wealth of the region out and leaving in its place desolation and the misshapen and the weak. I would change that by establishing a just regime over these mountains and, with that power, redress these wrongs." There was a wildness in his eyes. Being a subject of Greene would not be the ultimate in personal liberty. Surely the forces of the American government would stop this rebellion without delay and see that justice was done. Yet with these creatures, artillery, and a discontented peasantry, the task might be delayed until Greene and his associates, including the old artilleryman William Digby, were a force to be reckoned with. For his part, the Monster had the two things I desired: the notebooks and Felicia. An alliance with Greene for that end might be tolerable, but of what value would be his word?

"There are two things you must do if you are to leave alive," said Greene. "First, the formula, as I have said, and second, the elimination of the Monster."

"I am not a criminal," I said. "I have stated my reservations. Adding more to my misery will not lighten my load."

The stiletto began to glint before my eyes, and its tip was now upon my eyelid. I could feel it on the surface like a fly, starting to suck the blood. "Yield," hissed Greene, "or your last sight of this world will remain the memory of this storeroom."

"In the name of God, Greene," I whimpered. "Desist! Desist!"

"Yield, you treacherous swine!"

I could feel the point pressing in. "I yield!" I fainted

For how long I do not know. When I came to, I was lying on the table, with a bandage over my left eye. The lamp spun in slow circles as I watched and then came to a halt.

Greene's shadow fell back over me like a bad dream. "To the laboratory, Frankenstein. Instantly. That part of the bargain done, we will discuss the second."

I reeled along the outer passageway again to carry out my obligation. I had not slept for a whole day. There was no escaping, unless I would simply forfeit my life here and now. Getting in touch with the Monster, ostensibly for Greene's purpose, offered a possible way out, for if the Monster had his way and augmented his forces, his previous guarantee and his appreciation, perhaps, of Felicia's care during his convalescence might ensure the pledge. In the laboratory all was in readiness; Greene stood by with a smocked assistant and, finally assured of the simple step of reheating the result, allowed me to return to the storehouse where I had been tortured so that I could sleep.

"You cannot escape from the cave the way you entered, Frankenstein. The door of the chamber is barred. Rest. I will come by in good time."

There was no one in the chamber. The electric cells continued to bubble. With the fluid added and the electrical flow increased, the awful act of animation would be complete. I shuddered as with fever. I lay down on top of the table, snuffed the candle, and fell fast asleep, sweating at the burden of what I had done. It tramped in my soul like the sharp hoofs of horses.

CHAPTER IX

THE EVE OF RESURRECTION

THERE WAS the low sound of humming, as from a
hive of bees. It came from outside, toward the back of
the storeroom. There was a shaft of light, moonlight,
coming in from the top and back of the room. I rose
cautiously and slowly removed the bandage from my eye.
The bleeding had stopped and I could see. The damage
had been superficial, but the impact of that moment with
Greene would never leave me. Eyes adjusted to the dim
light, I could pick my way past the barrels and boxes
and at last, standing on the uppermost keg, could view
the outdoor scene. The moon had climbed again over the
highest ridge and was coating the trees and grass with
soft incandescent light. The whole community had assembled near the main entrance to the cave, and there
stood the Reverend Ritter, dressed in a flowing sheet
with his black hat on and his Bible clutched to his breast.
The flock too wore sheets, and all were lighting candles
by an oil lamp that blazed on a rock near where Ritter

was stationed. There was little breeze, although the opening was cool to my face. My field of vision was imperfect, and moving about on top of the keg did nothing to improve my view. Off to the west were bright flashes of lightning and dark clouds. But so far the storm seemed tied to the western mountains, and while its rumbles and lightning were freely shared with our Downs, not so the rain.

The white-clad throng, numbering perhaps a hundred, with their candles lighted, looked like a field of fireflies. There was a strange silence about the field, and Ritter, on the rock, seemed to be in a state of agitation. The hum of the crowd was followed by a murmur—a murmur of apprehension or appreciation. From out of a grove strode the Monster himself, also outfitted in a sheet, bareheaded, his square features stark against the moonlight. And following him, there could be no doubt, was the fair Felicia, after the manner of an acolyte. The throng parted and the Monster approached Ritter, who, stepping from the rock, handed lighted candles to both the Monster and Felicia.

Ritter then began to speak in an unnaturally high voice, which I recognized immediately as the work of alcohol. The Devil of Drink had him firmly by the throat. I knew not at the time what other devils might pursue him. I looked without success for Jenny, but in the sea of white it was difficult to make out men from women, let alone individuals. Felicia I could recognize because of her place by the Monster.

The sermon that Ritter was going to give could not be ordinary; I could anticipate its probable content. In his turnings from one part of the crowd to another, in the rising and lowering of his voice, I could not hear the sermon whole. But he recited from the Bible and he clearly had the audience in the grasp of his hand. "For verily I say unto you, that whosoever shall say unto this mountain, Be thou removed, and be thou cast into the sea; and shall not doubt in his heart, but shall believe that those things which he saith shall come to pass; he shall have whatsoever he saith."

He paused, unsteadily again, but his voice seemed to gain timbre and conviction. "The trail has been long to this wilderness, like the prophets of old in their wanderings and meditations. We come together again in the name of Christ, who is our Saviour. It is our belief in Him that has brought us this far. It is His gift that has sent us this extraordinary being, created by man in the name of God. He is without sin. He is our sure sign. Remember, Jesus said, 'Take heed that no man deceive you; for many shall come in my name, saying, I am Christ; and shall deceive many.' Now many were skeptical of the miracle of Jesus' rising from the tomb. He even asked them to come forward and touch the wounds on his hands and feet. For his believers anything is possible. 'And these signs shall follow them that believe; In my name shall they cast out devils; they shall speak with new tongues; They shall take up serpents; and if they drink any deadly thing, it shall not hurt them; they shall lay hands on the sick, and they shall recover.' "

The audience was growing more excited. Some miracle was clearly expected. Ritter went on, as though he had memorized the whole text. Had his mind been unclouded, the sense of the sermon would have been more precise, but at a cost in eloquence. I had failed in my mission, and he must have realized it. Hence to drink? But why then speak in such a certain tone? He must have decided that the only way to set things right was for him to be as clearly duped as his followers, so their rage would be directed toward the ones who had violated their good faith. The hypocrisy of the Monster in participating in Ritter's service heightened my hatred for him, for his guile, for his deception. Could I conceivably make use of him? This chain of ideas stirred my dissatisfaction with myself, tempered nonetheless by the fact that my range of option was small indeed.

"Now on the eve of our day of greatest hope, it is well to ponder the gospel and prepare ourselves for joy and meditation. It is not easy to accept again into this world those who have gone out of it. It is the ultimate test of our faith. After his crucifixion, 'Jesus himself stood in the midst of them, and saith unto them, Peace be unto you. But they were terrified and affrightened, and supposed that they had seen a spirit. And he said unto them, Why are ye troubled? and why do thoughts arise in your hearts?' To prove his existence as a living being, he thereupon ate boiled fish and honey, which we, too, have prepared for the glories of the morrow." There were more murmurs of approval from the crowd.

Ritter was moved by the spirit and the spirit of the alcohol to his greatest prowess. The throng joined hand in hand and a kind of personal electricity charged the moment to within an inch of explosion. "And what of tomorrow and what of the future?" asked Ritter, swaying about on the rock with his worn black Bible against his white robe, the contrast of the word and the lie. "Let me make known the word of the Lord." He held his Bible

to his chest and recited as though he were delivering
The Message, as though the Tablets of Moses were erected
well within his view and the revealed light of the Lord
was raining down upon him. Ritter called out in a loud
and tumultuous voice: "The Lord has revealed the future
to us, in his Book of Revelation. Think upon these words
and keep them always in your heart. 'And I saw a new
heaven and a new earth; for the first heaven and the
first earth were passed away; and there was no more sea.'
And I say to you, those friends and neighbors, sinners and
saints among us, who of us has seen the sea and been
afraid to enter it, even though it would wash away our
sins? Such cowardice stems from a lack of faith." This
drivel made little sense, but drew appreciative gasps from
the audience, like a fireworks display. "One thing we do
not need to fear is death, for Jesus has promised we shall
all rise again. 'And God shall wipe away all tears from
their eyes; and there shall be no more death. . . .'" And
here Ritter paused in profound significance. "'Neither sorrow, nor crying, neither shall there be any more pain: for
the former things are passed away.'"

From my precarious position I searched as best I
could the faces of those absorbing these moving words.
Isolated from reality, the words of the Reverend fell like
thunderbolts of yore and left a deep impact on the minds
of those who were within range of his increasingly me-
lodious voice. "The fear we have," said Ritter, "arises
solely from a lack of faith. And the beginning of faith is
that we love one another, as we loved, and will love,
those who are absent."

The sounds of thunder and lightning came over the
Downs as though they were orchestrated by the Great

Conductor. There was a freshening of the wind and a mighty rustle of leaves, like the approach of autumn or the Messenger of Death. Or the Goddess of Love. For with no further instruction, the multitude in white clasped one another in their arms and a mystery of mountain folklore began to unfold in my presence. The lack of a clear and complete field of vision in no way spoiled the scene. It was, alas, those very areas within my sight that left me shattered and weak within my prison.

Throughout this entire process the Monster had said nothing. He had kept his wretched countenance raised to the moon. The Reverend Ritter continued, his voice mellow with the fullness of the liquor and the fervor in his tongue. " 'And he that sat upon the throne said, Behold, I make all things new. And he said unto me, Write: for these words are true and faithful. And he said unto me, It is done. I am Alpha and Omega, the beginning and the end. I will give unto him that is athirst of the fountain of the water of life freely. He that overcometh shall inherit all things; and I will be his God, and he shall be my son.' " I dimly remembered the further admonishments that would have stilled, perhaps, the enthusiasm in this rustic throng, but to no avail could I call from my perch in a voice that would reach them, nor in fact did I have the desire to try to set them right. I counted only on the confusion of their mixed emotions and diverse aspirations to create the crack through which I could crawl and make good an escape.

The Monster was down on his knees, his great arms pressed heavenward, and the Reverend reached out to him and held his hand over his head in a gesture of benediction. Felicia arose, candle in her right hand, and comforted the brute with her left, stroking his crude strawlike hair. This stroking and fondling seemed a regular part of the worship, and the murmurs rose louder and softer at once. Suddenly the Monster rose and turned his massive body toward the throng and raised his great arms in a gesture of blessing.

There in the light of the candles and the moon, emerging from his sheet like a serpent, came the head of his throbbing erection. It was a sight that hushed the throng. His staff continued to grow as though it had its own independent existence. The end of his treasure was a pulsating purple, the fluid rushing to it like the rains to the river, and the sight of this tool, this primitive procreation prototype, for the moment awed his fellow worshipers. There was a pause and then a gasp as he seized Felicia in his powerful arms, and, with a grace and ease and religious solemnity, at once seated her on this throbbing organ. As she swooned, casting her flowing blond locks behind her, he moved off from the crowd, in the direction of his private grotto.

Before I could comprehend the enormity of this action, there was a wild cry and movement in the throng, and in an orgy as vivid as anything I had ever read about in Greek or Roman history, the entire congregation had paired off and were in couples, falling to the dew-fresh earth, working their will in a mighty offering to the gods of fertility. It was a pagan scene, without a redeeming sense of Christ or his works. Ritter himself, in total ecstasy, held a member of his flock in his embrace and in his frenzy spent himself before my very eyes. The vigil, it was clear, was to be throughout the night, with the expectation of the rite of resurrection in the morning.

I slumped down on the powder keg, shocked and outraged, shamed and disappointed over Felicia, and envious that I had been excluded from an event that boggled my imagination. I sat hot and panting for five minutes, then raised myself again with difficulty to gaze out on the Downs. The ground was covered by the white-sheeted bodies, as though a cloud had fallen and lay in bits and pieces over the whole of the clearing.

I tried to pull together the threads of reality. Greene was not likely to be among this group. His tight personality would not allow him to indulge in a public display of sex. He would have a problem, though, forbidding his men to avoid the scene, despite his misgivings, for the discipline that he and William had was tenuous indeed. These mountain folk, while peasants, had a degree of indifference and independence which made them difficult to control. Yet in some way Greene would have to rally his men for the morrow, when the struggle for power over these dismal Downs would perforce take place.

I could not think of these problems. My brain buzzed—it coalesced and congealed—over the awful sight I had just seen. No wonder the Monster had not raised his old demand for a woman of his own choice. His conversation, brief as it was, had indicated in retrospect that his desire for sexual release had been accomplished by his observance of nature, and that he had acted upon it—running beyond the mating of the greater animals, alas, to the understanding that the human vagina, in all its mysteries, would accommodate truly extraordinary challenges. This was all well enough on an impersonal basis, but what of the outrage I had just seen, my betrothed carried away like meat on a spit, to the admiration and appreciation of the most lascivious people in the world? I had fixed my eyes on them in the moonlight the best I could, seeing the young and the old, the blemished and the unblemished, straining their bodies the one to the other in the frenzy of Ritter's message of love and resurrection. Those scenes and recalled faces would clog my brain forever, no device for erasure having yet been presented. Felicia defiled. How could I ever again look upon her as my partner for life, my lover, my wife? She would be, as I had been, mortified by this occasion. Clearly she had not sought it, but neither had she resisted. She had glided onto him as a shank of lamb seeks the skewer. How could I ever forgive, forget, this blasphemy of biological relations? This was not so much a question of being unfaithful—she might accuse me successfully as well—as being a partner in blasphemy, in animalism if you will. To lend her sex to forbidden enterprises—and worse, I had to confess, in public. I grew red at the thought.

My requirement now, as before, was to find allies to do battle with these forces of evil. The alcoholism of Ritter was one thing, but his debauchery was another. He had made a mockery of the cloth, like the popes of Rome, and my marginal foothold on the cliffs of religion slipped away altogether. On the dawn, however, Ritter would arise from his bed of sin contrite and on his knees to the sun, from which all blessings would flow. In his hatred for the flesh he would be the first to abuse it. He did still control the thoughts and hopes of the congregation that he had persuaded in the first instance to settle on the Downs. And he had armed the male members. Fifty rifles would answer to his summons. The forces of Greene were smaller, but there was the advantage of another kind of purpose, not connected with the soul. It was the lust for power and authority, two qualities that Greene and his lackey, William Digby, relied on to carry forward their grubby cause.

Or so I saw it. It was difficult to place the Monster's power in this perspective. Clearly his word was law, and neither Ritter nor Greene openly opposed this. His isolation arose, in the eye of an outsider, from his inhumanity, and while he must have thought that everyone, including Ritter and Greene, was a willing member of his fiefdom, a deeper analysis might have shaken his confidence. True, Greene and Ritter were frightened of him, Greene because he feared that the Monster would realize Greene's own aims, and Ritter only because he was losing confidence in the Monster's assurances. The Monster's move to the side of one or the other would clearly tilt the balance. Or on the morrow, if the creatures were responsive to his direction, the balance of power in this tiniest of principalities would again be altered. It was a frightful scene, and anyone fully realizing it could not spend the night asleep. It was to my advantage that the many possibilities were not in fact widely recognized. There arose, therefore, the possibility of shifting the balance of power in a direction favorable to myself.

The lull in the battle would not continue for long. The animation of these grotesque organisms would take several hours, and the forces of Greene were clearly in charge of this. They would soon resume their grisly work. I took advantage of the pause to go into the main laboratory where the vile bodies lay. Here the sparking of the wires between electric cells and bodies was more pronounced. There were a glow and hum in the chamber, a sense of growing activation, that frightened me. I still wanted to warn Ritter of the morrow, with the hope that his sex-satiated tribe would somehow behave in a heroic manner. There was no guard visible, but the door leading back toward my original entry point was bolted. There was no hope in that direction.

I drew near the closest table, where a white sheet covered the entire form. All that was lacking, I assumed, was the addition of the animating force of the fluid which, in concourse with the electricity, would cause these monstrosities to rise and go forth to the greater glory of whoever would henceforth control them. The light in the chamber was steady but dim, the pine torches, lanterns, and oil lamps providing an eerie light. With caution I pulled back the sheet from the first form. While I had been prepared psychologically and mentally for shock, I reeled in terror and fright. My collapse was complete, my hopes blasted. For there in this light, as I gazed on another countenance as ugly and nonhuman as that of the Monster, were the open eyes and the black hair, fastened with a mother-of-pearl hairpin, of Jenny. A gross body had been constructed from the raw materials of this foul assemblage, intermixed with Jenny's features, and her eyes stared up at me as if to speak. They were sunken in outsized sockets, as though from a cow or deer, but those eyes, though contorted by death, were still her eyes, and the black hair, which covered the massive blocklike head only partially, was still as soft as the silky tresses I had clung to only the previous night. The tears and shudders from my body would not cease.

So Greene knew. In his rage he had destroyed his wife. What control he had, what need he had, that he constrained himself with his evil stiletto so that his grand design could be carried out. I had already filled one of his demands, and now the elimination of the Monster was to be the second. Greene had known of the ritual I had just witnessed, the orgy on the Downs. Some other victim must have been impaled on the mighty root of the Monster on previous occasions. And Greene knew that my hatred of the Monster, before now on an impersonal, even theoretical, level, would rise to new heights—that all the wrongs done to my father's family would come to my mind like steady drops of water, and, with the rape of Felicia, drive my mind from its feeble moorings. Greene no doubt hoped that with this sight before me I would race from the cavern and throw myself on the Monster, both of us perishing in mortal combat. And so I might have, had I not come across Jenny. I would go from the cave, yes, but not just yet. It might well be that there were no restrictions on leaving the cave, since anyone inside presumably had entered with Greene's approval. I could not see the entrance from the observation hole, so I did not know what the guard situation was at the moment. Had the guards participated in the orgy that was still in progress?

What if I were to try to stop this evil experiment at its inception? Suppose I were to disconnect the electrodes? Try to destroy the electric cells? I felt powerless, completely powerless. There were sounds now of people walking into the next chamber. They must be the small band of trusted helpers Greene would now require to inject the fluid into these misshapen but powerful forms. How many would he animate this night? He would need enough to alter the power balance against Ritter and the

Monster himself. The Monster must not so far suspect treachery on Greene's part. Was that the reason for Greene's wanton, insane killing of Jenny? Had she in despair threatened Greene? Our secret had perhaps not been shared.

As the sounds grew closer, I moved quietly back into the storeroom and sat on the chair to which I had previously been bound. The oil lamp was almost out, and I found a supply of candles. I lighted one by the oil lamp, and as it burned I dripped wax onto the table and then set the candle upright. The flame was true and burned steadily, with no sputter and little drip. I sat staring at it for a while, my mind blank. I removed my gold watch and placed it on the table. Then my mind began to function again. Agitated, I marked off the candle in lengths of the top joint of my thumb. And I watched. It took fifty-three minutes for the first joint to burn. There was a slight taper to the candle, so the second would burn longer. It did, by ten minutes. It was now midnight. Daylight would be around 6:30, the sun rising behind the mountains and dispelling the light clouds by perhaps eight. That would seem to be the most dramatic moment, the first rays of the sun pouring into the valley. Or there might be no detailed planning, the animated creatures proceeding when ready. I could hear a scuffling about in the outer room, where the creaking wheels of carts told me that these gross objects were being moved off to the smaller laboratory for the transfusion of the fluid. This could be done quite quickly, much faster than in the case of the Monster, whose system was already functioning and could not be overloaded.

I took up a large, fresh candle and marked off what

I thought would be eight hours, right to the base. Then I moved quietly up through the storeroom to my previous lookout. The revelers were still on the ground like moths and apparently would stay there the rest of the night. I returned to my work. It was with difficulty that I found a place where I could light the candle with a sulphur match and secure it where the light of the flame would not be noticed from the table. By placing it near the opening, the moon might for the moment provide that protection. I broke open the top of the keg of gunpowder, making a fine but adequate line to the base of the candle. If it were undetected and did not blow out, this evil place would be destroyed, stone by stone.

I had no more sat down in the chair, perspiring, than the door opened. A draft stirred the candle flame on the table as the ventilation quickened throughout the room. Greene closed the door, with a thrust of his arm. "I will soon release you, Frankenstein, in line with the second part of our agreement."

"I am faint, Greene," I replied. "Why use me? Just take your guards, led by William Digby, and kill him in his sleep."

"Not quite as simple as that, Frankenstein. The guards do not know of my plan, and I am not yet ready to tell them. Digby would not be able to accomplish the task himself. And an attempt that failed by Digby or me would be the end of all this work."

"But how am I to accomplish this formidable task?"

"You are a dangerous and clever fellow, Frankenstein. You have in the past tried to murder him by poison. You are a murderer in the sense that you have already committed the crime of putting the arsenic into the fluid, knowing for whom it was intended. That it failed to work does not erase that stain from your rotten soul. I leave it to you how you will murder him."

"A pistol, then, or a knife?"

"I myself quite doubt that a single round of any conventional firearm would with certainty finish him off. A knife? Your hand would tremble and it would clatter to the ground. I know this. If you do not make the attempt, you and your lover will be dead. I will send you on your way. The dispatch with which you act is your surest road to your return to the society for which you yearn. With the dawn your life will be your own responsibility. You are not welcome here, and you will be fired upon on sight, hunted like a rabbit, and your neck wrung with no more concern, though there would be less use for your dark hide."

Greene allowed himself another hollow laugh at his cleverness, and the even yellowness of his teeth was reflected in the candlelight. I buttoned my coat and inadvertently touched my injured eye. It was scabbing over and again Greene smiled sardonically. "Come. We are to leave. I will place this small black bag over your head to spare you any sights that you might find offensive." That done, he led me from the room. As the door opened, there was another feeling of a draft that could jeopardize my plan. Perhaps I had become a murderer, for I no more cared about the fate of whoever might be struck down than for Greene's rabbit. In striking down my enemies, it might, in so doing, carry away friends. But how in this impersonal world could the explosion know differently? Like me, it would do what it must.

The squeaking of the carts continued, and the hum

of the water wheels increased as we walked through the large room, through another door, and then into silence. Greene removed the bag, remarking how well it fitted my head. There were pine torches ablaze at intervals of perhaps twenty yards, and within five minutes we were at the cavern's entrance. Greene took me past the guards, then right, skirting the sleeping multitude, although some of the number still continued their sexual play. Greene walked on briskly, past the storehouse and a row of houses now deserted by the occupants for the Downs, and to a grove. "On through here is the den of the Monster. There too will be his dog and Felicia. I am confident that you will see him destroyed with as much glee as it will give me. You have promised and sworn that you will undertake this task as a condition of your release. Quickly done, you, along with your paramour, will be well away by dawn. You will do me no harm, nor I you. Our lives have crossed but briefly, and need not do so again."

He motioned me to the path through the grove and I went ahead blindly. My ambition to enter the lair of the Monster was motivated not so much by Greene's threats as by my own insane desire to find those notebooks and then make good the escape. Trying to collaborate with the Monster was simply too risky. If I did not kill him, he might in the last analysis be the final barrier to escape. If I tried to persuade him of Greene's treachery, he would either not believe me or force me to help him forestall Greene. No, better that he were safely dead. Greene was, after all, a less formidable enemy.

Felicia. I did not know what I now thought of Felicia, her lovely moss-covered grotto contaminated by the tracks of this offal. I tried to press those thoughts from my mind and alert my senses for the dog. He was an intelligent beast and his last memory of me would be a piece of meat that did not settle well on his stomach. In the moonlight filtering down through the heavy early autumn leaves, I found a fallen branch, which, with a minimum of effort, became a potent club, then spotted a stone the size of my fist. Thus armed, I advanced like a cave man against one of the strongest and most sinister forces alive in the world. I had gone fifty steps when I saw the path turn into a clearing. There was the trickling sound of water, and I could see the reflection of the moon in a natural pool. The beauty of the spot was unsurpassed. I moved as silently as the moon, my senses at their keenest, expecting at any moment to have to deal with Prince.

As I entered the shaded end of the pool, in the moonlit portion, not twenty yards away, out stepped Felicia, her golden hair streaming down her back, eyes lifted to the moon, her breasts tilted upward and her naked thighs glistening from the pure spring water. The sight was breath-taking. I wanted to take her up and place her on the dewy grass and ravish her. But the image of the awful scene of just hours before choked off my desire like a pair of sinewy hands, and the dichotomy between desire and shame nearly split my brain asunder. Instead, I approached her at the edge of the pond with only a whisper, "Felicia, Felicia," a muted sound that I still hear in the night. There was no fear on her part. She came straight to me and threw her arms about me and covered my face with kisses. "Oh, Victor, Victor. I'm so happy that you have come. I'm terribly frightened. Now is our opportunity to go. The Monster sleeps. Let us go at once from this evil place." Despite myself, I returned her embrace, but not with my usual ardor and she could tell. "What is wrong, Victor, darling? What is wrong?"

"Our task is not yet finished," I said. "As part of my pact with Greene, I must first immobilize the Monster. That done, we are free to go. It will also be safer. What happens if he wakes? He would track us down in a moment."

"Immobilize him?" she asked incredulously. "What does that mean?"

"A potion. You did meet Greene's wife, the woman Jenny?" I asked.

"I did indeed. She was agitated beyond herself and left with me two potions and the pistol. I placed them beneath my pillow, and my sleep has been disturbed ever since."

Again I took her into my arms. She began to tremble as did I, for opposite reasons. "There is little time," I said. "If we are to make good our departure, you must give me your devotion."

"I do, Victor, I do." She nestled herself into my body, and except for my humiliating experience earlier that evening, I would have ravished her at once. "The problem in leaving centers on the Monster. Tomorrow is an important day, an occasion I can only surmise." I felt her naked body shudder. "And if we can be far away before then, our nightmare will be over."

"What must I do?"

"You must secure me in the den, administer a potion to the Monster that will leave him asleep for a day, and put aside any inquiries as to my whereabouts while I am in the den."

"Victor, my darling, I will do as you request. There is no life for me beyond loving you. I have suffered here, that is true, but it is bearable because of you."

If she would only confess her misdeed! If she could say that she had been mesmerized and victimized! Not one word. Would she expect at a later date, safely my wife, to confess a portion of her sexual misdeeds with the Monster? Was that her plan? Or was she expecting to follow the course of her life without revealing to friend or foe the extraordinary violation of her privacy? But there was the immediate problem of Greene, and so I suppressed these painful thoughts and asked, "Can you tell me of his habits in the morning, now that he is sound, so that a sleeping potion can be delivered effectively?"

"Victor, I would suggest that his first cup of tea would do your service. It is strong and filled with sugar and milk. Which packet shall I use?"

I hesitated. "The yellow one. Yes, the yellow."

A shadow crossed her eyes and was gone. "I love you, Victor darling. And I trust you."

At this moment I noticed in the light of the moon the extent of her full and agitated bosoms. I was again tempted. "Take the potion in the yellow wrapper and place it in his cup. Stir it in before adding the sugar and milk. That will do the task. Once he is definitely out, then we will prepare to leave. I will remain concealed until then. Do not reveal my whereabouts to anyone who may inquire."

We kissed and kissed and kissed again. Despite my

aversion, my passion rose, but at the moment of decision, Prince arrived, coming smartly from the den, shoving his muzzle up close to Felicia's private parts, growling in a low, questioning way. Satisfied, he left for his duties in the grove.

"I will do as you require, darling," said Felicia and, grasping my hand, led me into the cave. There was little light, save for an oil lamp on one wall, the light being as dim as the fires of hell are hot. The Monster was stretched out on his pallet, in a deep sleep of love and victory. In the back of this single chamber, there was a confusion of goods and neglect. Under this heap I crawled. Felicia blew me a kiss, dressed, and assumed her role as administrator to the needs of the Monster. It was now three o'clock. Time was short, and the dawn of the day of resurrection was at hand.

CHAPTER X

TREACHERY

IT HAD BEEN my intention to remain alert, hoping that the Monster would soon awake and the potion be administered. Exhaustion instead triumphed. I awoke, startled by the rumble of voices. The entrance to the Monster's cave showed that the first light had crept down the obscured rays of the sun, crossing the clouds in the mountains. The dark golden hours for escape were gone, and I was now fair game for Greene. I was nonetheless well concealed, and, saving a slip from Felicia, the situation still might be retrieved.

"Has Frankenstein been here?" asked Greene in a harsh whisper, which carried through the chamber despite his intentions. Had he thought I would have risked an immediate escape, contrary to my pledge? "Yes," I heard Felicia say, in her most fey voice, which carried a good deal of conviction. "And has the necessary been done?" he inquired, entering the cave and carefully watching the sleeping figure of the world's most diabolic being.

"I know not what you mean," she responded.

Greene weighed her reply. He scratched his head, tilting his round hat to an absurd angle. Had he assumed that I would ask Felicia's help, as indeed I had, merely to "immobilize" the Monster? To have suggested to Felicia that the draught was deadly would have been to forgo the effort. Her innocence was her last virtue. I had, alas, discovered that. Had the Monster taken from her hand the bitter herb tea which concealed the laudanum and arsenic? She would in time realize that it was necessary, that a simple sleeping potion was not the answer. My only regret was that I did not have hydrocyanic acid, which would have settled the matter quickly and certainly. I had seen only a few cases of such poisoning, the widely dilated pupils, convulsions, disturbed rhythm of respiration, the bluish countenance. And death—in minutes. Given the size and strength of the Monster, my method was risky. Yet it was all I could do.

Greene now directed his close attention to the Monster. He moved to his fur-strewn pallet, placed his strong bony fingers on the Monster's wrist, and gingerly opened an eye with his other hand. "He's dead. Thank God he is dead. But why did you not flee with Frankenstein?"

Felicia held her ground. "The Monster is not dead. He rests. As for Frankenstein, he attended the Monster, then left, saying nothing of an intention not to return."

Greene was puzzled. "If Frankenstein lingers here, he may have difficulty. But let us fret about that later." He again held his hand to the Monster's wrist and his ear to his chest. "He is indeed dead. This is a great relief," he said. "No human was safe from him."

"No, no!" cried Felicia, throwing herself on the Daemon. "He sleeps, he sleeps."

"As you wish," said Greene, looking about the room. He moved as if to investigate the far end of the room, near my concealment, but instead smiled and leered at Felicia, laughed his hollow laugh, and was gone.

Immediately upon Greene's departure, Felicia came to my hiding place. "You heard, Victor, the words of Greene. Is it possible that the potion I applied in his tea when he rose from his slumber is fatal? Is it possible that you have deceived me?" There was a growing hysteria in her voice.

I rose from the litter of my hiding place and attempted to placate Felicia. "The potion from my medical bag I have given a thousand times. It is a laudanum derivative that produces deep sleep, not death. Greene is not a doctor. If the Monster's pulse is low, it is only because that is normally so, and this has lowered it still further, so that to the uninitiated he appears dead. He will, however, revive all too soon. It is that probability wherein lies our greatest peril." I could not tell her the truth.

"He does appear uncommonly pale and weak," said Felicia. "His vigor had returned, and if I had not your assurance I too would judge him assuredly dead."

"I dislike this turn of events in that I have now on the same foggy morning twice been accused of murder. The Lord told Peter that before the cock crowed he would be betrayed thrice. Is there someone else yet to denounce me?"

The bite of my remarks did not escape Felicia. "Victor, for too long have all of us been required to accept the world as it is and not ask why it is this way. Those of you who are physicians have a double duty to heal our minds as well as our bodies."

I looked cautiously out the entrance. "Had I not slept, we should have been gone. All is not yet lost in any event. The Monster will rise again. It is in this moment, while Greene has left and before the sycophants of the Monster appear, that we can make good our escape."

"Dear Victor, I know what you say is true. While the Monster's sleep appears exceedingly deep, and I am, in truth, concerned about his recovery, I shall prepare to leave—though little needs to be done."

"Who is likely to appear here early?"

"That is not fixed. And today is special. But perhaps William Digby. William usually comes to see him. They often talk long about politics and money and other subjects in which I have little interest. With the excitement being generated over the anticipated return of their loved ones, though, who can predict? In that regard, dear Victor, I find that prospect difficult to believe, despite the Reverend Ritter's eloquence and cleverness with the word of God."

"In the presence of the Monster himself, we know the proof of the process of animation. But the remobilization of dead bodies in their previous form, when by definition their dead bodies could not stand the ravages of disease, a bullet, or what have you, seems unlikely."

"Then what is the recourse? Ritter's people are here only for that purpose, and if they are disappointed, there will be bitter and deadly recrimination."

"That is correct," I said, "and for that reason we

must make good our escape while Greene is preoccupied and before the Monster arises."

Felicia looked again at the Monster oddly, skeptical that he lived—also, I thought, with both compassion and admiration. Lust, no, yet the memory of the previous evening, her being carried upon the lance of this foul Fiend, spread a deadly feeling of contamination into my very soul. I could hardly touch her. I sat heavily on a bench, nearly swooning.

"Victor, are you ill?" she asked.

"Perhaps a fever," I said. "The old storehouse is not so far distant," I added, "that perhaps you could retrieve my medical case on the pretext that the Monster wants it."

"You require the case?"

"I had best take what items will be of value. It may take us several trying days, or longer, to find ourselves free of this place. During that time we shall be at the mercy of the insects and animals and the elements. It would be a sound precaution."

"I'll try," replied Felicia, still brooding, and went out the entrance.

This was the moment I had waited for. I would never leave the Downs without making this one supreme effort. My ruse so far had worked. Now to find the notebooks. As the light improved, I could focus on the details of the cave. On the walls were great crude murals on the face of the rock, made by fiery strokes of charcoal, expressing the frustrations and feelings of the Monster as he contemplated a world that rejected him, and one that would try, however vainly, to conquer him. Then there were religious artifacts, dominated by a huge crucifix, realistically done, but without a trace of artistry, that hung over his crude sleeping platform. I recoiled from the thought that Felicia had shared his bed. The place was rank with the smell of uncured furs and stagnant water and dog stools. Around the perimeter of his bed were strips of cloth bearing the imprint of his purple, royal blood, providing me with another index of the loss of the fluid that had slowed his powers before his cure. He lay still on the bed in an ever deepening sleep. His face now had a deathly pallor which would have frightened Felicia. I felt his pulse. It was so low that I too would have thought him dead.

The Monster groaned and turned in his sleep, and fear again paralyzed me. If his stomach was empty, the arsenic would take hold more quickly; otherwise, it would be slow. And if he suddenly vomited the whole mixture, he might still recover. My impulse was to find an ax and cut off his head, something that would be unequivocal, for I had witnessed too many scars on his body from wounds that should have been fatal, but that in one way or the other were patched up, leaving him free to recover and again menace my world. I did not, however, see any such tool at hand, and in the time remaining to my plan, I was determined to recover the notebooks and leave the Monster, Greene, William, and the Reverend Ritter to their mutual destiny. Felicia certainly would return any moment. The next few minutes, therefore, would be my only chance.

At the far end of the cave there was a desk of sorts, a kind of primitive workbench with boards thrown over a pair of simple sawhorses. I started toward it slowly, keeping a close eye on the drugged and poisoned Daemon, not really trusting that he was that far gone, fearful that he was only lying there, resting, waiting for the right moment to kill me with a mighty wrench of his hands. I was at last next to the desk and looked about carefully. There were no drawers, so if the prize were at hand, it was buried beneath the mementos of things past that covered the desk: medical orders, exhortations to Greene to be passed on to the Reverend Ritter, simple notes on the next day's schedule, and a kind of diary. "Rev. Ritter and Greene paid their respects to the Widow Bailey. They discussed the certainty of death and resurrection, and requested her support and the body of her husband, as uncontaminated as possible."

There was another stir and groan from the Monster, and I froze before the desk. I turned as slowly and silently as possible. I looked again for a weapon—my club even —to administer a coup. I approached the platform again. His eyes were tightly closed, and the veins stood out strained on his forehead. His features were exhibiting great tension. Still in all, the quantity of laudanum and arsenic was working. Every minute increased the probability that it would be fatal. If I were wrong, I would pay for the error with my life.

I felt the pulse again. The wrist felt lifeless, like picking up a dead tree limb which had lain in a pool of cold and stagnant water. Yet the pulse was steady, and God alone knew what it might take to still that gross body. I could not speculate in this way any longer, if I were to discover the notebooks.

Again I walked the half-dozen paces to his desk. There were some books, mainly on religious subjects—

the *New Testament,* Saint Augustine's *The City of God,*
and some science books, including a well-worn copy of
Harvey's *The Circulation of the Blood.* I carefully lifted
each item on the table as though it were a precious jade
carving to see if, as I expected, the notebooks would be
there, like *The Scarlet Letter.* Next to Moses' tablets,
these notes were surely the most important written work
in human history. But there was absolutely nothing there
that I wanted.

I returned to the pallet of the Monster. His breathing was almost imperceptible, although there was a kind
of grin, both wild and friendly, on his face. Was he going
to come back, against all odds? Yet there was no sign of
consciousness. I was determined to look longer. I gazed
down on his hideous features with an ambivalent feeling
that severed my soul and body as neatly as if someone had
split me like a log, with one blow of an exceptionally
sharp ax. The pallet was in foul order, smelling and stink-
ing like the Monster now lying on it, and in the general
disorder of a refuse pit. Again the vision of Felicia despoiling herself addled my brain.

The notebooks! The notebooks! I doubted that the
Monster would carry them on his person. He would have
to keep them well hidden, especially from his disciples,
or they would seize that information and continue the
work on their own. Greene no doubt had that very much
in mind and would make their recovery his first order of
business, after the resurrection. Good God, that would be
less than an hour away! There was little time left. Felicia
would soon be back. I could not enlist her aid in the
search. Hers would be the same view as Jenny's: let them

be. And there was also the matter of making good our escape. Would my delay mean that I would trade my life for the chance of finding the notebooks?

Time was pressing on. The Monster was beginning to stir. Where were the notebooks? I abandoned the workbench. My eyes darted from one place to the other, seeking inspiration. In sheer frustration I threw myself against an enormous rock near the entrance to the cave. It turned slightly but easily, and there under the stone was a metal box, fitted tightly into a dry crevice. The lid lifted easily, and there was the Grail that had for so long filled my dreams. It was only a single notebook, but even a casual skimming of the pages left no doubt as to its authenticity. I placed it in my oilskin and stuffed it inside my coat pocket.

Then there was suddenly the answer to my problem with the Monster. I had, in casting my eyes about the room, largely ignored Felicia's simple bed, although something about it had momentarily attracted my attention. Then I remembered. I reached inside the pillowcase. I found the second and harmless potion, the one in brown paper, and, at the bottom, my pistol! I checked it. It was loaded, ready to fire. I hastily wrapped it in her thin blanket and, with trembling hand, once again approached the sleeping and poisoned Monster. I placed the pistol directly over his closed right eye. The lid did not quite make a perfect fit, but no matter. The round would find his brain and that would be the end. I thought I heard footsteps, but, hoping to still the sound with the blanket, I steadily squeezed the trigger. There was a click, which sounded in my ear as loud as an avalanche. But no concluding shot. Misfire! I threw the pistol and the blanket to the ground, moving on outside, ready to take Felicia and run. It was 7:30. If the explosion was to occur, it would be soon.

I stepped out of the cave into the early morning sun. To the west was a spectacular blue-black line of rain clouds moving our way. Felicia appeared and paused in confusion. By her side was William, who held in his hand a percussion pistol. His face was as dark and threatening as the oncoming storm.

"Hold, Frankenstein, right where you are. Is murder to be added to your crimes against social justice and common decency?"

Felicia burst into tears; she did not come closer, as I had expected. She covered her eyes, and her shoulders shook slightly. She dropped the medical bag to the ground.

"Your leader is in his bed, resting," I said. "I am here with the permission of Mr. Greene. And with his explicit permission, we are now making our way from here."

"I know of no such understanding, Doctor," he said. "And to prove my openness of mind, let us go this moment to Mr. Greene, who will, if you are not misspeaking, verify your claim and send you on your way. But before then, Felicia has confessed that you may have tricked her into administering a poisonous potion to the Monster. Come into the cave, and if that is so, you will work to revive him. If for any reason he dies, his end will be yours as well."

"He is in his bed resting," I repeated. "I know nothing of this poison charge whereof you speak. Nor does Felicia. She is merely distraught." Had Felicia not been there, perhaps I would have told William that it had been done on Greene's orders, but this explanation was denied to me. "Finally, I am not accustomed to being ordered by my man to do his bidding."

William pointed the pistol menacingly. "You will do as I say, Frankenstein."

I came forward two paces under the threat of the waving pistol. "Do you really fear for the Monster, or do you plan to take his place, your ambition soaring on beyond your position in this world, power having corrupted your former integrity?"

His answer was violent. "You are a victim of your own mad ambition, Frankenstein. The one who is trying to be the king of the monsters is no one other than yourself. And you would go to any length for that end."

I continued forward. "Felicia, darling, don't be afraid. The Monster is all right. I have assured you. I don't know why you are so upset. No one means him any harm. He is all right. See for yourself."

She lowered her hands and came to my arms. And before William was aware of what had happened, using Felicia as a shield, I moved toward him an additional pace and kicked the weapon from his trembling hand. As he clutched the hand in pain, I recovered the pistol. I turned to him and, with all the hatred that I had accumulated toward him, I struck him with the palm of my right hand on the tip of the jaw. His head snapped back and he fell to the earth unconscious. With his own belt I tied his wrists and ankles together and dragged him into the cave.

"My God, my God," moaned Felicia. "How will this all end? Is everyone against everyone else? Is there no sense of common interest, only murder and power?"

"Felicia, we must go quickly into the pines and then move on down toward the river. We must hasten from here while there is time." The revelers had again assembled and folk religious songs new to my ear rose in the valley. Felicia followed me readily enough through the trees into the rocks of the first ridge, about one hundred yards from the mouth of the entrance of the laboratory cave. We lay down in a protected place. We could not quite see the entrance, but we were as close as I felt secure. Felicia was silent. I could not determine by her attitude whether she came this far out of concern for me, concern about us, or simply because she did not know what else to do.

"Victor, you must tell me the truth. You tricked me, did you not, into poisoning the Monster, after you had given me your solemn word that you would not take his life?"

"What you gave to him was laudanum, which will only make him groggy," I lied. "Let us speak no further of it."

"You are angry with me, Victor. Admit it."

I said nothing.

"I can tell from your expression, Victor, of your anger and shame for what you either saw or heard about . . his seizing me, forcibly, while I was in a trance of the Holy Spirit or from Ritter's words. I regret that, Victor. God has forgiven me. It was only my body, Victor. You know how I love you."

"But why did you say what you did to William, about my poisoning the Monster?"

"I did not mean to. When he approached me and suddenly demanded to know of the Monster's condition,

I told the truth, that I was worried, and the rest followed. Despite your assurance, I was still not sure. When I thought I had been tricked into killing him, you must understand that I was stunned. I now believe you, darling. Please understand and forgive me."

I held my tongue. Never again did I want to hear of the poisoning. But the assault. To look at her, she was the same Felicia as ever. The orgy, her hour of reveling with that bloody Monster, had not changed a line on her face. She was in her own mind my moral superior, having sacrificed only her body and not her soul. Whereas in her eyes, my rage to murder the Monster—reduce him to his murky origins—for what he had done to the Frankensteins and for what he had done to Felicia was so morally repugnant that she had difficulty reconciling herself to me. Could she not see that my forgiveness of her would be a greater sacrifice for me than hers of me? That her sexual soiling would burn in my mind however I tried to extinguish it? Paradoxically, though, my obsession with her golden body was so great that I wanted her now more than at any other time in my life.

"What is happening now, Victor?" asked Felicia, suddenly alert as she pointed to the sheet-clad throng, many holding bouquets of field flowers. The crowd was falling back, and a low wail of sound, of agony and disappointment, began to swell in the Downs and rise across the ridge into the heavens in protest. The Reverend Ritter, holding his Bible aloft like a shield and a sword, alone moved forward, with a mighty cry, "Deceivers, devils all!"

At that moment, one could see fully half a dozen of Greene's and the Monster's creatures lurching into the sunlight, raising their ponderous arms and hands to shield their eyes from the sudden brightness. There was a moment of absolute silence as before a storm. And into that silence came a sucking sound and then a great exhalation. The whole ridge around the cave shuddered, swelling up to twice its size, sending stones and boulders high into the air and then collapsing upon itself in a pile of total rubble. Wild cries arose from the injured, and in the midst of this suffering, there was the sound of rifle shots. They came from the grove to the east, where Greene's guard was collected, and in return, amongst the carnage, Ritter's men began to answer.

"We must flee, darling, while there may be time." The sound of rifle shots was increasing in intensity. But no artillery, which would have left Ritter without hope, assuming that he had survived the explosion. William was still tied in the lair of the Monster. Felicia did my bidding, and we climbed quickly up the first ridge, sliding down the rock-strewn slope to the stream and on into it. The waters had risen remarkably during the night as a consequence of the storms which continued in the far end of the valley. The wind was freshening from the west, however, and those same storms would soon be upon us. In my oilskin were the few simple supplies: water, matches, jerkin beef, and the priceless notebook. I had not bothered with the medical bag, it having carried me as far as I could reasonably hope. I regretted throwing away the pistol, but with no ammunition it would have been worth-while only as a stage prop, and would hardly have fooled anyone in the drama that was unfolding.

We waded knee deep in the stream for about 100 yards,

slipping and bruising our legs, but, in the inevitable hunt, this might save us more time. As we stumbled out on the far bank, however, a plan finally began to form in my numbed brain. The boats. The path cutting across the stream was no more than three or four hundred yards down-river. We could wrestle one of those primitive craft into the water and follow the current to safety and civilization. The gamble would be whether the sentry box Ritter had mentioned was still manned at the confluence, for if it were, we would have no chance at all. Whether it is right to be rash or cautious is a judgment of history, the victor inevitably making the right choice and the vanquished having let his opportunity slip by.

Near the boats I left Felicia in another pine bower, which brought jabbing pain to my brow as I thought once again of the cruel fate of Jenny. There could be no sense of forgiveness in Greene. I had done his bidding and then more. The explosion was something he had not expected, and once again in his hands, my life would surely be forfeit. Exhausted from the past two days, I moved slowly down the right-hand bank of the stream. At the confluence there was indeed a sentry box. And beside it were three of Greene's guards, busily heating hot water for their morning tea. Despite the sound of firing, which was quite distinct, they were obeying their earlier orders to stay at their post. Had they been of heroic mold, they would have joined the battle; instead, like ordinary men everywhere, they preferred to do their duty.

I returned to Felicia, described the situation, and outlined my best hopes for escape. Though the sound of gunfire was still intense, sleep overpowered both of us. We awoke from the silence. The wind was bending the pines. The black clouds were low over the valley, moving quickly toward the east. There were great bursts of lightning flashes, not yet the roar of thunder, but ground lightning that illuminated here one spot and there another. Just below the solid clouds were streaks of clouds, like torn tufts of cotton, just clearing the trees. And over the river were swarms of bats, feeding on the insect harvest that was being blown along. The rain could be but minutes behind. I looked at my watch. Just six. Yet it was as dark as night. The river was a growing torrent, and a new sense of fear assaulted me.

Who had won the battle? Perhaps our fears were ended. If Ritter had won, there was nothing for me to do but to return and help the wounded. Concluding this odyssey on such a note would be anticlimactic but welcome. The simplest check would be of the sentry box, but in this weather it would be difficult to see whether the guards were from one faction or the other. The odds, however, were in favor of the crafty Greene, foreknowledge being worth an extra twenty men. I would forever wish to escape any kind of machinations, although the knowledge of the notebook in my oilskin was not the best guarantee of such a long-term outcome. Huddled in the dark, startled by the lightning and now by the advancing thunder, I held Felicia, soiled but irresistible, in my arms.

Then through those rolling sounds came the yips and howls of dogs on the scent. The baying was of the bloodhounds that played a part in the outer security of the Monster's plateau. The Monster's side—that is, Greene's side—must have won the battle. Ritter would not have organized such a search party—nay, hunt party.

I shook Felicia fully awake and led her to the boats. The first one we struggled into the water and I deliberately let it go, to see how it behaved in the water and also to eliminate another means of pursuit. It rode high in the water and within minutes disappeared down into the black and plunging current. The second we placed into position near the edge of the rising stream. I only then returned to secure the one simple paddle left with the boats. The second boat was harder to launch, for we had to drag it over a large rock and lost time in getting into the boat. Felicia was sorely afraid, and my reassurance was not altogether convincing. The leaves and pine needles helped lubricate the path and we were ready to depart.

"What of the Monster, Victor? Do you think he will pursue us?"

"No, Felicia. Do not worry about him."

"Is that because he is dead?"

"All right," I said. "I have had enough. Yes, he is dead. No one deserved it more."

"My God," cried Felicia, staring at her hands.

There was then the lull I had been expecting, as the forces of nature gathered themselves for the final assault. But in that moment, a row of torches appeared over the ridge on the opposite side of the river. In this solemn silence, there came the voice that turned my spine to liquid, the deadly metallic voice of the Monster, enraged.

"Frankenstein, you poisoner and murderer. You mass executioner. You are a blot on the name of mankind. Release the girl and surrender yourself to justice."

"Wretch," I challenged, in a voice that carried back up the bank with great clarity, "don't moralize to others.

You are the antichrist, the devil of the world. You and your evil cohorts deceived the simple folk of these parts, and if I have helped to thwart your foul plans, so much the better. You besmirch everything you touch. Be gone with your thieves and murderers and let us go in peace."

My attention was so drawn to the Monster that William was almost upon me from the rear, seeking to crack my skull with his flaming torch. I avoided the blow, which showered sparks over the rocks and into the water, wrestled the torch from his grasp, and with a powerful kick sent him headlong into the river. There was another cry of rage from the far bank.

I held close to Felicia, waving the torch, knowing they would not yet fire if she were before me. She was frozen, immobile in her tracks. With an inspired thought, I next hurled the torch with all my strength straight toward the voice and the angry knot of men. It carried the stream and set off the dust-dry pine needles as though they were gunpowder. "Now, Felicia, now," I cried and urged her into the bow.

For her answer she stepped instead into the rushing water. "You liar, you deceitful liar. You did poison him, through me. You blew to pieces innocent people. And you would continue to corrupt me. It is you, and not the Monster, who is the spirit of evil." I called her name again, but the boat was suddenly freed by the rising waters. She fell amongst the rocks in the water and I was gone.

The heavens opened and the rain came down so hard that it obscured the pursuers, who had been driven back up the bank by the blazing fire. Going past the sentry box, I knelt low in the boat, but there were no rifle shots. I pushed myself further into the current with my simple paddle and safely joined the main river, which was exhibiting the characteristics of rage that were swelling in my chest. Only now was I beginning to understand what Felicia had said and what all that meant. I looked back, and against the backdrop of the flames, which had so far survived the rain, I saw the silhouette of the Monster pushing off in a boat with a giant pole, probably a pine that he had torn up by the roots.

I had a lead of at least one hundred yards. Miraculous as his recovery was, the experience of being poisoned could not help but weaken him. I counted also upon the difficulty of the river and the lighter draft of my boat to help at this critical moment. In the meantime, I paddled on either side of the boat as though possessed, even though the current by now seemed to be carrying the boat as fast as possible, so that my paddling effort was wasted. I resolved to use the paddle like a rudder to stay in the fastest section of the current and thus to handle whatever exigencies arose.

These exigencies came much faster and with more challenge than I had anticipated. I had never experienced anything this spectacular in Scotland. As the stream filled and the heavy rain continued, the idyllic nature of the river of yesterday turned to a scene of growing alarm. As mighty streams of water were compressed through narrow rock passages, they became powerful chutes, and the rocks that before looked like loose dice from a pagan gambling game now lurked just above or below the surface and hissed like dragons as one passed them in the pitch-black night. I could not recognize much in the changed landscape because of the growing width of the river. Suddenly there was another magnificent display of lightning, lighting the heavens, the mountains, the forests, everything under creation. To my left, caught in this incandescent spectacle, was the huge cross at the place where I had camped the first night. And on that cross hung the crucified body of the Reverend Ritter, his black hat and white sheet still on his body and an enormous dark stain down his chest.

CHAPTER XI

THE CHASE

MY EYES were blurred from the rain and the tears. I wept to the mood of heaven. But fear won over sorrow and I strained my muscles to their outer endurance. In the moment of quiet, the river was a great dark torrent, flecked more and more frequently by white as the waters rose over most of the rocks and began to re-create the rapids that had disappeared in the summer in the heat of the sun and the long drought. Pitch-black was the river, but lighted, sometimes too well, by the fiery streaks across the entire valley, so that every rock and crevice in the river was held up to close inspection by the forces of Nature. And to the eyes of the Monster, who, I knew, was in close pursuit. Much as I wanted to know whether he was overtaking me, I looked ahead and paddled, surprised each time I went safely through the growing turbulence of the rapids, which were becoming almost continuous, scooping out briefly, as best I could with my hands, the quantities of water that splashed over the gunnels.

Here and there bushes and trees would grab at me and the boat from the shore like so many clutching hands; but with the rise of the river, it was increasingly easier to stay further from shore—only, however, at the danger of the growing violence of the waves and turbulence arising from the rock-strewn bottom of the river. After twenty minutes or so, there was a sharp right-angle bend to the left and I was fortunate to steer my boat to the inside, for had I gone further over, it would surely have swamped in the standing waves and have been crushed against the bank. As I made the turn successfully, I looked back upriver. Again silhouetted against the sky, the great forest fire now raging toward the heavens, were the Monster and his boat. He had knelt for better balance and was poling furiously, and he had succeeded in closing the margin to not more than sixty yards. But before I was able to concentrate on that threat, there was a decided change in the river ahead, as it began to fall even more sharply. And there in the next flash of lightning I saw a series of ledges and chutes that defied my previous appreciation of the river. If I had any kind of mishap here, the Monster would be upon me and the whole project, the whole point of my taking this enormous risk, would be lost. The oilskin was still in my soaking coat. The chances for its survival were better than mine.

In the most agitated places in the rapids giant holes appeared in the water, frothing and gurgling, churning in awful whirlpools, six feet across and as deep, waiting to snatch and suck down the boat and boatman in a watery embrace. Each one I passed I prayed that it would seize the Monster, but each time I arrived at the end of the wild turbulence and cast a backward glance, there was the Monster kneeling in his craft, still pursuing like the daemon from hell he surely was.

I took the passage to the left of a boiling boulder in the center of the stream, hugging over toward the larger boulders leading toward the bank. The lightning flashes irradiated the whole scene, and in one blinding flash I saw that I was going to collide with a low, flat rock. I leaned in toward the rock, knowing that a backward lean would fill the boat with water and leave me at the mercy of the elements and the Daemon. As it was, the boat slid off the rock and the bow nosed into the eddy behind the rock, which spun me about in a dizzying fashion and left me shaking behind the boulder. From there I could see that the next section of rapids was even more violent on the left side going downstream, and that a safer course would be on the far side of the river, if I could manage to ferry my clumsy craft across the ever quickening current. The current in the eddy flowed directly upstream, and by keeping my hand on the rock I was for the moment safe. My heart was in my mouth, however, for if the Monster came the same route with the same result of eddying out of the stream and finding his way to the base of the rock, the race would be over and I would lose my life along with the awful secret of the creation of life. I crouched in the shadow, afraid to try to look beyond the rock to check on the progress of the Monster. At that very moment, the Monster and his craft came shooting through the rapid, his giant pole seeking purchase on the rocky and slippery floor of the river as a cane seeks the friendly support of the cobblestone. His face was set directly ahead, and I caught no sight of his eyes. His hair was matted from the rain, hanging down his checks and the back of his neck. His ear stuck out like a dorsal fin. He was having difficulty keeping afloat, and he was striving to guide toward the left bank, either to rest or, more likely, to see if I had left the river and had fled on foot.

This was precisely the course of action I had resolved against. Once out of the protection of the river, paradoxically, this tumultuous torrent of foam and rocks, I would be in an even more vulnerable position. I could not hope to outrun him, or hide for long against his acute sense of scent and hearing, as well as his great speed. He went on toward the left and about thirty yards away was able to stop the boat and scramble off onto a rock, holding the boat and drawing it in front of the rock into a smaller eddy. He sat on the rock, his back to me, searching the river and the shore line, as the heavens shook and the lightning rent the skies into terrible tatters, and the thunder sounded on and on and on and rolled away in the distance like a rock slide. Nay, like the roar of the explosion at the cave this very morning.

The thought of that explosion moved my mind temporarily beyond fear, back to the Downs, and I was amazed at how many thoughts could tumble through my mind in the time it takes for a zigzag of lightning and the rumble of a clap of thunder. My whole involvement in this affair, the scene in Aunt Margaret's library, William extending his silver tray with the card, "Frederick Greene, Chandler, Baltimore, Maryland," the sherry, the fire, Greene's odd features, the experiments with the fluid, Felicia. Oh, God, Felicia! How I had failed in my trust! How I had misused her bright spirit in the name of the end result! Instead of blaming myself, I had instead blamed her, faulting her for events outside her control and from which I should have spared her in the first instance. And I had abandoned her among the rocks of the river, leaving her life entirely in the hands of the Monster or Greene, in the far reaches of civilization where she would at best lead a nasty and brutish life, but which she preferred to the prospect of life with me. Like King Midas, I had a fateful touch, only in my case spreading death and disaster. I thought of throwing myself into the river and ending the whole affair. But even that good I could not do.

My position at this moment was quite safe. The Monster could not see me, sheltered as I was inside the eddy. And in the midst of this storm, he could in no way backtrack up the stream to seize me. On the contrary, a bold maneuver began to fill my mind. If I could finally kill the Monster, I would settle the family score once and for all and avenge my irrevocable loss of Felicia. The evil in this Monster's creation was not my father's but rather that of the Monster, however cleverly he denied it, however winningly and cunningly his logic struck. If he were dead, I might even prove just that point, not having to explain or argue about the potential for evil in such creatures if they are imprudently produced or if they somehow escape their proper station and are allowed to walk the earth in imitation of man.

There was no obvious way out of this narrow valley, and if he continued on down the river ahead of me, he would sooner or later decide on some strategic location guarding a narrow gorge, for example, and pounce upon me when I passed. So waiting behind would not resolve my problem. No, better to come to terms with the alternative now. I carefully placed in the bow two rocks, each about one stone in weight. I hefted them and they felt adequate. The Monster remained with his back toward me, looking forward intently, or perhaps listening, except that the roar of the river blotted out of my ears everything but the explosions of thunder as the autumn rain released every fluid ounce, like a primitive orgasm.

I knelt on the bottom of the boat and pressed my knees against the bottom of the gunnels. Then I shoved the bow just to the edge of the current, at the eddy line, and started slipping my way from my hiding place. The eddy was so strong that I had to paddle vigorously to make progress toward his rock, careful not to go toward shore too far so that I would come up from the left instead of the right, but also not to get into the surge of the current, which would take me past and far to the right in a matter of seconds. By now I was closing, fifteen yards, ten yards, then five.

There was no way he could possibly have heard me, but as I steadied the boat, laid down the paddle, and raised the rock, he began to turn slowly upstream. And at the moment when I was releasing the rock with all my might, he raised his gigantic arm and, in a brilliant flash of lightning, deflected the deadly blow. It struck his arm and grazed the top of his head, causing him to fall back into the water. The second rock caught him on the right shoulder solidly, and he started to sink beside his boat. Just as I grasped my paddle for a *coup de grace*, his mighty head came up out of the water, with the purplish fluid streaming down his face. With a roar that rose above the storm and the tumult of the water, he came toward me. I shoved off the rock toward the current, and his great hand scraped the very side of the boat. But I was away clean, my mission unaccomplished. I had not been able to kill him. The battle had swung to his side. Despite the grievous blows I had scored, he was alive. But his boat was gone into the current! He had no way to pursue me further. Then as if by magic, there in the same eddy, half submerged, was the first boat I had released. He raised it triumphantly in the sky, shook out the water, seized his pole, and again was in pursuit.

The second series of major rapids was more terrifying than the first. And with the Monster at such close range, any misfortune on my part in the rapids would deliver me into his power. I could feel those powerful steel-like hands about my throat and the final brutal shaking and twisting as he wrung my head from my body. I thought then of throwing the oilskin into the river, so that if he did seize me, the secret would be gone. Someone might find it later, but without the knowledge of what was being discussed, it would probably be safe enough as a kind of odd curiosity. But I had put too much into it. This is why I had taken such risks, why I had been blinded by the power and had misused Felicia. I would not part with it.

Now I concentrated all my mind and strength in moving through the rapids. The sky was beginning to clear, and the moon began to light the way. But what a way! The rapids hissed as they picked up intensity and there was a suctionlike sound as my craft just missed the round but deadly rocks in the path. The rapids now looked almost solid white, and in this dim light it was impossible to identify a safe channel through them. Accordingly, I followed the longest downstream tongue that disappeared somewhere down in the turmoil and headed toward the largest waves. That was where the deepest water should be and where the safest course would lie. This was carrying me far out into the middle of the river, and the next bend would cut on back to my left. Kneeling again in the center of the boat and using my knees to maintain the stability of the craft and the paddle as a rudder, I was making exceptional progress. The sky was light enough to see the waves and steer clear of the deepest troughs and the highest waves, which I approached at a slight angle to avoid the full shock. I longed to look back, but it was simply not possible to do so safely. My salvation lay, if anywhere, in my skill at keeping afloat and in remaining as far ahead of the Monster as possible. Though this rapid was half a mile long and created exceptionally high waves, I saw a safe channel off to my left and took it. The moon again came out, and a blood-curdling sight met my eyes. The Monster had gone directly downstream, ignoring the prudent channel, and was now bearing down on me. His face was contorted with effort and pain. He was not more than twenty yards away. A surge of strength hit my system as though on call only for this occasion. I slashed the paddle into the stream with savage furor, striking a rock and hopelessly jamming it between two submerged rocks. The force of the current tore the paddle from my hands, and the boat spun about so that I was now going downstream backward. The Daemon poised for the kill, bringing his great pole out of the water and starting its descent, which at that moment I welcomed. I was too spent even to fall out of the boat on my own energy.

As the blow came down, there was a great crunch and the Daemon's boat stopped as though in mid-air. The pole flew harmlessly by, and the Monster was pitched headlong toward the center of the stream. I grabbed up the pole; it was almost too heavy for me to handle, but it did give me steerage, and I pushed as fast as I could to outdistance the Monster. He was swept far out into the current and through heavy waters. I lost sight of him for the moment, but given his strength, there was no reason to believe that he would perish, unless he was injured more seriously than I believed. The water was becoming calmer except for the center current, and I was able to catch my breath and stand in the boat and survey the scene. I did not know for certain where the stream would debouch. I eased toward the center, with a sharp eye for my enemy. Each rock took on the appearance of his square and ugly head. Each ripple spoke of his powerful swimming strokes. I looked back and forth as if I were swinging a lantern so that he could not surprise me. And in so doing I undid myself.

My hearing was numbed from the roar of the river and the sequence of events. As I looked straight ahead, the river took on the impression of a table edge, a line drawn across the river. And in that instant I realized where the end of the river might be—the giant falls at Berkeley Springs. Within fifty yards the current had the boat in an iron grasp, and the sound of the tons of water falling onto the rocks below became a muted roar. And then out of the black, ten yards to my right, I heard the voice. "Victor, save me. Frankenstein, Frankenstein!" I thought of striking him with the pole, but I feared he might seize it and somehow throw me from my boat. Instead, I pushed forward with redoubled speed. There was nothing else to be done. At the edge of the falls, I rode along the end of the V at an accelerating pace, poling once, twice, three times. The boat began to fall away and fill with water. With one final thrust, I flung myself out as far as I could to avoid being sucked up in the hydraulic maelstrom below and being ground into bits like driftwood. The sensation of falling lasted for what seemed minutes. Then a crack of a leg on the rocks, a pitch forward into the boiling turbulent waters, a feeling of suffocation and silence.

CHAPTER XII

THE FLAWED ESCAPE

I AWOKE in a simple white bed. My left leg was in splints and was throbbing. My body was bruised everywhere I touched. The sun was bright and high, and there was a certain familiarity about the room that strangely excited me and created a sense of apprehension. I leaned on my elbow toward the window. I was on the second floor of an inn, with a vast circular drive leading out to a highway. There were no sounds other than the birds, and I could not see features beyond the drive that would positively identify the name of the establishment. And in the room, there was no sign of my clothes or the precious oilskin!

Then I knew exactly where I was. It was the Berkeley Springs Inn, the main part and not a cottage. The falls must have been the one I had seen earlier when William and I had ridden past leaving Felicia behind—Felicia! how the thought of her brought sweat to my forehead—and I had somehow been cast up, like Jonah from the whale, and had been rescued. But the oilskin. Where was the oilskin? If the notebook was lost, I had failed in my mission. Worse, the information was lost, lost forever. Either way, however, I had to know. First, I would make inquiries when the nurse or doctor came, to learn if it were not somewhere in the inn. And if it were not, I would go myself to the falls, once my leg and body and brain were mended, and search for it. I had had a glimpse of the power of the notebook, and it was a sight that despite my loathings was not easy to dismiss from memory.

I lay immobilized in the bed, eyes fixed to the ceiling, and perspiration glistened my brow. The pain in my lower leg was tolerable enough if I remained perfectly still. Then it was a slow, steady throb, and if I could have kept my brain dormant as well, all would have been bearable enough. But such is not the nature of human enterprise. My brain began to grow feverish when the real events poured over me, wet and cold like the last moments of the ordeal of the waterfall. The Monster, the Monster! What had happened? I remembered his call and plea just short of the falls. My final thrust of the pole had thrown me clear of the churning whirlpool at the base of the falls. But I could not foresee how any fate would fall to him but that of a log, spinning round and round in the garden of rocks, removing layer after layer, until a shapeless pulp of purple gore would wash on down the stream, the food for fishes and for crayfish and other scavengers that would rise for this unsanctified bait.

Or he might have been salvaged from the river like a broken boat and lie in this very inn, also with wounds and broken bones, and creating a medical sensation as doctor after doctor would be summoned from near and far to marvel at this monster man, the scientific achievement of the age, already corrupted beyond the measure of mind to treat with it.

But my brain was still overwhelmed by the vivid recent events, as though here and there it had been paralyzed. The scene on the Downs! Jenny's grisly fate, the wild orgy, the conflagration, Felicia's betrayal, the Reverend Ritter's crucifixion, the power of the river, my narrow escape from the Fiend and the water. I wanted to scream out in protest against loading the human facility with more than it could bear. My hands gripped the thin mattress. And then the door opened.

I don't know what I was prepared to see. But the sight of a slight girl, of normal dimensions and a bright smile, was the best omen I had had since, well, the last time Aunt Margaret had smiled at me over tea.

"You are awake," she said cheerfully. "How do you feel?"

"Fairly well, thank you. My leg throbs, but that's to be expected." I paused. "What may be hurting most of all, I think, is my poor head. I mean I really don't remember a great deal and I want to know."

"You do remember being washed over the falls?" she asked.

"Yes."

"But nothing more?"

"Not really."

"You remember nothing about the fishermen pulling you out and bringing you here?"

"Nothing. And what of my clothes?" I dared not yet raise the question of the oilskin.

"Your belongings are here, in this closet," she replied.

"And what's there?" I pursued anxiously.

"Why, whatever you had, I suppose."

"Bring whatever is there, please."

The girl did as I asked. She opened the closet door, which swung in my direction, blocking the whole thing from view.

"Well, there's not much here. A torn shirt, trousers, a jacket, a heavy belt."

"What else? What else?"

"Something here in the corner . . . just some rags."

Of course, the oilskin was in the jacket! "Bring the jacket to me, please. And everything else."

She brought all the damp debris. I feverishly stuck my hand into the coat pocket, but it was empty. Gone! My money belt was a small consolation, for it assured me of a return to civilization, a passport to a happier era. The lift of this idea, however, did not compensate for my dejection over the disappearance of the oilskin. It was not likely anyone would steal something of that kind. More likely by far the money belt.

"What is the matter, sir?"

"Nothing, really. But I wonder. This is asking a bit, I know, but would you be good enough to go over to the falls and search around the pools and eddies along the bank? There may be a chance that a simple oilskin packet, waterlogged but basically intact, is there. It contains various biological notes, and botanical notes as well, the results of my expedition. I would be devastated without the notes. If I lose them, then I think I will be lost too."

"The river waters are high, sir, and if you lost an oilskin packet last night, it would be most unusual to find it here. It would likely wash further down."

"But you admit it is possible, do you not? I'll suitably reward you." I arranged my visage in its most appealing manner.

She did not answer me, however, but averted her eyes, her face clouded over like a late afternoon on the Downs. She gave a slight curtsy and a curious smile and turned to open the door as the doctor entered. This was no prescience on my part. The faint smell of ether, the black bag, and the expensive clothes—frilled collar, brocaded hat, winning grin—all marked him beyond question as a member of my profession.

"Dr. Saville?" he asked brightly.

"Yes," I replied. How soothing that name sounded! Had it only suited me, I would not be lying in this bed in this strange inn.

"I am Doctor Wheeler. The break was rather nasty, but I think the set is good and the splint is tight. To be sure, you'll have to be off the leg for several weeks and use crutches."

"I feared that. You mean I'm confined to this inn?"

"There are worse places," he smiled. "The food is tolerable, and you'll mend quickly. You must be charmed to have survived the falls. I've lived here for over ten years, and I do not recall anyone who has gotten off as lightly as you."

"It was something of a miracle," I said. "Few have lived to tell of it, I assume."

"Yes. . . ."

"I mean, few have lived through the experience. Were there other survivors?"

The doctor was puzzled. "Were you not alone?"

"I was quite alone. Yet, in my fright, I thought I saw someone floundering in the river."

"That's curious. I have not heard of any other casualties. A hallucination. Before you leave, you may feel up to describing that plunge. The falls have always fascinated me, drawn me to them. And I fear their power."

My leg began to throb again, and perspiration broke out on my forehead. Dr. Wheeler gave me a large and potent dose of a sleeping potion. I lay awake another half hour, nonetheless, wondering whom I could persuade to conduct the search for the oilskin, until sleep fell on me like a boulder. I saw sparks from a fire, a burning cross, and heard the roar of a gigantic rapids.

It was twilight when I awoke. There was still a profound silence over the grounds, but humanized by the smells of ham and greens cooking somewhere below. My door opened, and another young lady entered, dressed in a white jumper and green blouse, the serving uniform of the inn. She left for me vegetable soup and a lighted candle, not thinking that I was really awake. I pulled myself up further in the bed and ate some soup, which acted as a miraculous restorative. My mind cleared. I looked out the window again. In the near distance I heard the clatter of the stage on the turnpike, and within minutes it entered the sweeping drive and the horses snorted up to the inn. There was an interchange of shouts and crude jokes and curses as the four horses were changed. Mail packets similarly moved each way. No one disembarked. The work was done within ten minutes and the stage was off, the lanterns beaming brightly.

After eating I used the snuffer to extinguish the candle. I lay back again, becoming distraught and longing for Felicia. I prayed that God would find some way for us both to forgive each other. I could forgive anything or anyone at this moment, join forces with the Devil, to be certain that the Fiend was once and for all stamped from the earthly scene. The exhilaration I had briefly felt upon hearing that he had not been rescued was tempered by the prospect that the notebook was in other hands, and the whole cycle could be renewed by some of nature's greatest scoundrels. That secret was the responsibility of the Frankensteins, and although I shuddered from the prospect, I could not shirk my duty.

Sometime later during the night the door opened and a large shadow fell over the floor, exaggerated by the hall light into a fantasy of frightening dimensions. I was aware of the rustle of a gown and then a shadow over my bed. I sensed who it was. Felicia! Her hand, white in the darkness and near her throat, descended slowly and ominously toward my chest. Was this the last act of her recrimination?

She shook my shoulder gently. "Victor! Victor!"

Should I shout for help? But who might respond? "Felicia," I said thickly, "you've come to me."

At that she fell upon my chest with a mighty sob and covered my face with wet kisses. I enfolded her in my arms, and we clung together, warm and close and safe.

Her tale was a simple one. She had been carried by the stream several hundred yards. The spectacle of the Monster in hot and mortal pursuit of her rejected lover had in one instant illuminated her mind, and she had realized that the Monster was in fact the essence of evil and that her denunciation of me had been a grievous error. She had been assisted to safety from the high plateau by remnants of Ritter's followers, and had regained the village of Berkeley Springs on horseback this very evening. At the inn, where she too was staying, she had heard the story of my adventure, and at the earliest opportunity she had entered my chamber.

"Darling," I said at length, "my heart is once again full. It had dried up and, I feared, would never swell again."

Her sobs continued but at last were spent. "I shall make up for my faults, my darling. That I could have doubted your integrity is a sin I shall bear with me to the grave."

"Let us talk of life instead," I answered. "We must make plans to flee this place. If Ritter's friends could come this far this soon, other forces may not be far behind."

She quivered in my arms. "Victor, you are right; we must leave this inn on the morrow. But how can you move? Should I secure the services of a rustic to help you from the bed to a carriage?"

"The stage comes here," I said, but paused. This would be the obvious route of retreat, and if the Monster, or Greene more probably at this juncture, were in pursuit, the stage would be his first target.

"I believe I have it," I said at length. "We should make one more bold stroke and thus secure our sanity and freedom."

"What am I to do, Victor?"

"Two things. First, at dawn go to the riverbank below the falls and carefully regard each pool and eddy to find the oilskin pouch within whose folds rests the secret of life's creation.''

"No, Victor," Felicia sighed. "Recall your vow that our goal was to forsake this place and leave the riddle of life behind, lost for all eternity."

I felt feverish. "All I ask is one brief glimpse. If it's not there, then fair enough. We go. The second task is to find a private hire, a man and carriage who will speed us hence by nine o'clock. The stage comes by at dusk. We'll be away before the Greenes of this world know what we are about, and in that unexpected gain in time will lie our own salvation."

"I gladly will obey the latter wish, dear Victor, but I would ask you once again to forswear the search for secrets that are best unfound."

"I do not ask it lightly, dearest. It still means much to me, my father's son, enough to ask for one last search, one hasty glance, to see if this historic work may, in proper hands, lighten man's burden at some future time."

"Very well, Victor, I shall do both as you demand, with fervent prayer that both ends are accomplished as you desire."

Our souls unlocked, I slept the remainder of the night like a dead man. Then the brightness of the sun brought me back to the reality of the inn. Felicia was gone on her twin mission. With that in mind, my appetite improved and did full justice to two poached eggs, blueberry muffins, and a pitcher of milk. This was delivered by another maid, the natural homely variety, the breeding problem, poor teeth, thin complexion, and watery, intense eyes. There was a birthmark over her left eye, with hair growing out of it. But even her unsavory appearance did not deter my spirits. I finished the breakfast at a leisurely, sensuous pace and lay back on the bed to await the return of Felicia.

A troubled Dr. Wheeler arrived instead. He looked as though he had not slept for days. I waited anxiously for him to speak; but he had difficulty catching his breath, so his message was delayed. Had it only been possible for it to have been forgotten completely!

"A bizarre and terrible event has befallen a guest of the inn," he said in a somber voice.

I raised myself slowly and painfully. "Where—and how?"

"Down by the falls. Her head beaten in by a rock."

There was only one head, one fragile, exquisite head, that he could possibly be describing. I knew it like the chapters of the Bible.

"Murdered? Felicia McInnes? No! No!"

"I do not know her name. A blond, petite guest."

I was horror-struck. The doctor pushed me down on the bed and held my shoulders.

"Who in the name of God," he asked, "would murder an innocent girl in cold blood?"

Who indeed? From what I had seen of this evil place, I would judge that half the people in the region might do such a thing. Yet in my heart the number lessened to those who wanted what she may have found. Dr. Wheeler talked on, as though in the distance, about the body's having been partly submerged in water, but death was from a blow to the head and not from drowning. So my desire, once renounced, had risen like a viper and struck my love. Oh, wretched beast that I was! Love had lost once more, through choice. How could I err on such a vital thing? Why could I not let reason rule my world?

I lay back on my pillow as Dr. Wheeler adjusted my splint. If the notebook was again in hostile hands, I would still be required. Because of the explosion, there was surely no one left who had grasped the idea of how to manufacture the fluid. Everything still led back to Frankenstein, like the twine in the labyrinth of the Minotaur. If for no reason other than my own safety, I must have it.

Dr. Wheeler was preparing to leave. "A tragedy indeed, Dr. Saville. A flower plucked before its time, to die and wither. The town is shocked."

I buried my head in the pillow.

"You knew her well then?" he asked.

For answer, my sobs shook the bed. I knew her—yes, Great God, I knew her.

"I'll return tomorrow," the good physician said, as though speaking through a depth of water. "If I'm needed before, kindly dispatch the maid."

On these words the maid materialized and removed the plates. She cast a curious glance in my direction, undoubtedly noting my features, wild, distorted as they must have been. I lay back and closed my eyes. Then, like a kaleidoscope that suddenly clears, I recognized her face. There was that very face, the livid birthmark and blush, in the upper corner of this obscene painting, making love with one of the white-sheeted rustics, screaming with joy and salvation. And as I remembered, she was associated with Greene's faction. Felicia's death foretold too well the danger in this sunny place. I too was wanted. I was helpless and now alone, prey for the weakest antagonist.

I lay in the bed as though paralyzed for perhaps an hour. My brain simply would not function. I had been through too much—too much had been demanded from my physical system to rise to yet another occasion. All on my own I could tell Dr. Wheeler of my suspicions and fears and be jailed as the accomplice who sent Felicia to a damp and early grave. The cook! Jenny had mentioned that the cook would vouch for me upon presentation of the hairpin, which I was now using to keep my robe in place. But what would I tell her? What could she do? Or suppose I appealed for protection from the village constable. Given the determination of my enemies, even that would not save me from being kidnaped and held for whatever dark purpose was in the shadows of their evil minds. Greene's offer to release me had not been an unconditional guarantee of safe return, especially after the explosion—although which of their number were dead or alive following that event and the subsequent battle was a point for conjecture. That they had struck down my love was a grim warning.

Weary as I was and frightened, from somewhere again came the will to live, the desire to escape, a lust for vengeance perhaps. Whatever it was finally brought me to the peak of my senses. I would save myself. First, I wiggled one of the bedposts and found that it was notched into place none too securely. The rest would depend upon whatever fate decreed.

Lunch was pork chops and an apple. This contributed to an awkward wrestle with the bed pan. I catnapped on through the afternoon, ringing the bell for my supper a bit early—good peanut soup, freshly made rolls, fresh corn, and roast venison. My appetite was not yet that

strong, but once the maid removed the plates, I felt reasonably certain I would be left to myself.

After she departed with the tray, I sat up in bed and
drew the chair from the table to the edge of the bed. I
moved over onto the chair, taking care to secure my
broken leg horizontally on the bed. I slowly shook the
bedpost loose, so that the bed sagged down but did not
crash to the floor. Then I slowly, slowly rose from the
bed, using the bedpost as a crutch, and keeping my left leg
as horizontal as I could so that the blood would not rush
into it and so that it did not touch the floor.

I had my money belt around my waist, and the
pinned robe flowed like a Roman toga. I made my way
toward the door. The pain was fierce but bearable. The
sky was becoming purple, and the woods and trees took
on a mottled appearance. The stagecoach sounds came up
the valley from a great distance. I should have just enough
time.

As I stood balanced within three feet of the door, I
saw the porcelain knob move almost imperceptibly. Perhaps it was not even moving, just a trick of my eyes and
strained nerves. Yes, yes, it was. I reached out with my
left hand and leaned against the wall, so that when the
door opened, I was behind it. I stood like a heron, waiting
for the intruder's entrance.

The hall lamp cast a shadow on the floor of a shape I
would recognize in the next world. It was the round rim
of Greene's hat, like a dark moon. It was fitting that this
bizarre and untrustworthy personality, murderer of his
wife, had been the first contact I had had with the Monster's organization. My kidnaper and jailer, he would
now be the last. My bedpost impacted as he stepped for-

ward, stiletto drawn. The crash of Greene and me to the floor was partly muted by the commotion of the arrival of the stage. Lying atop him, I felt his pulse, which was still strong. I pushed him over on his back and, with a mind numbed beyond measure, unpinned my robe and plunged the mother-of-pearl hairpin into his open right eye. Jenny was revenged, and possibly, if revenge meant anything, so was Felicia.

For what seemed an eternity, I blacked out from the pain of my broken leg and the horror of Greene's silent body. But it must not have been more than an instant. I hastily felt his pockets to determine whether he had the notebook in his possession. Nothing. And I had wasted a precious minute. Then I was back on my crutch and out into the hall. I feared, however, at each step, that I would faint away and never descend the long staircase into the lobby and waiting room.

Again there appeared to be no passengers for the coach, yet my escape was still in the balance. The coach-men were already on their seat, and the two outriders had started on ahead. I lurched out the main entrance in mighty hops, grasped the coach-door handle, and shoved myself in, the bedpost rattling to the gravel. I lay panting on the back seat of the coach as it left with a jolt. There were indistinct cries, but the stage continued onward, the wheels grinding loudly on the drive.

I sensed the turn down the mountain and felt the coach gather speed. The pain of my throbbing leg was sending me into unconsciousness. I looked up and out as we passed a narrow place with dark trees hanging low on either side of the turnpike. There was another lurch as a heavy object landed on the back of the coach. A metallic voice sounded as though it were in my ear. "Frankenstein! Frankenstein!" I shuddered. I knew once more beyond question in whose hands reposed the accursed notebook.

The end was near. He would overwhelm the stage, killing the drivers and sending the horses flying, hurling me on a final fatal journey over the nearest precipice. I welcomed the prospect. Anything to save me from his clammy grip, his oyster eyes, his sanctimonious words as he choked the life from my broken body. The horses slowed, whinnied, then reared and leapt forward. The great weight was released with a thud onto the cobbled pike, and the coach rolled free on down the mountain.

The pounding of my brain obliterated counterclaims from my damaged leg. I was no more my own master than a caged bird. I could flutter about and chirp. Or I could bide my time, aspire to become a eagle, return to these dark slopes, and clear the name of Frankenstein.

The image of Felicia's face in the moonlight seemed to smile as I remembered Romeo's words:

> O my love! my wife!
> Death, that hath suck'd the honey of thy breath,
> Hath had no power yet upon thy beauty:
> Thou art not conquer'd; beauty's ensign yet
> Is crimson in thy lips and in thy cheeks,
> And death's pale flag is not advanced there.

I resolved that her sad fate, if left unpunished, would be my own, and that of mankind. Thus composed, I slept. The coach wound its way toward Washington, a new land, a new life, a new demand for final justice.